The Journeyman:
An Apprentice's Tale

Cover design by Getcovers
www.getcovers.com

Table of Contents

Life is a luminous pause between two great mysteries that are yet one—Carl Jung

Call of the Void

I felt the panic rising before I stepped off the elevator. My palms were slick, and my legs trembled faintly beneath me, as though the floor might fall away at any moment. I checked the floor and room number again: second time, third time—hoping I'd made a mistake. But no. This was where I was supposed to be.

The corridor was quiet, but not still. A man shuffled toward me in a faded gown, head bowed, muttering softly to no one visible. Behind him, another figure sat slumped in a plastic chair, unmoving. His thinning grey hair stuck out in tufts, and his face was slack, his eyes vacant, staring into the darkness. I couldn't tell if he was old or simply hollowed out—worn thin by the ravages of his own thoughts.

A chill crawled over me. I had never been inside a psychiatric ward before, but my gut told me that's exactly where I was. There was a sterile stillness to the place—not the healing kind, but the kind that made you feel forgotten.

I passed through a set of heavy double doors into a long hallway that could've belonged to a dream. The walls were white, the floor a shining checkerboard of black and white vinyl that reflected the overhead lights so perfectly that it created the illusion of walking inside a mirror. I found the door. Dr. M. Chan, Psychiatrist. A black nameplate with white letters.

To the right of the door were two chairs—identical, black vinyl, metal legs, as lifeless as the hallway. A small black table sat between them, holding a few ragged magazines whose curled pages whispered of time wasted and nerves unraveling.

I sat. The chair felt harder than it should. I glanced down the corridor—endless pairs of chairs and doors repeating themselves into oblivion. No windows. No clocks. No sense of time. Just the quiet hum of fluorescent lighting and something else—a faint pull beneath the surface of things, as though the air itself were telling me to leave.

Four months on these damn drugs and now this. My doctor had run out of explanations for the panic attacks that kept crashing through me. This time, instead of another dosage increase, she said we were entering "specialist territory." That meant a referral to the General Hospital—to a psychiatrist.

What she didn't mention, not once, was that his office was located on the psychiatric ward. She knew. I had told her—more than once—that I was terrified of losing my mind. That I feared being locked away, misinterpreted, medicated into silence. She knew I was barely holding it together. And still, she sent me here, like I was a problem to be passed along. I couldn't shake the image: being strapped to a bed, eyes pleading, voice ignored. Words pouring out of me only to be met with more pills. More fog.

A patient appeared through the double doors, slouched forward, eyes fixed blankly on the floor. His hospital gown hung loosely, gaping at the back. The patches of pale, exposed skin—weathered and unguarded—were a mirror I didn't want to face. Was this my future? Was I already this far gone? I was on the verge of bolting for the elevator when the door opened and a tall, lanky Asian man in a white doctor's coat stepped out.

He looked at me calmly—too calmly—his eyes tracking the patient as he shuffled past, lingering a moment too long. "Come in," he said, without looking directly at me.

"Please sit down." He gestured to a black chair, identical to those in the corridor. He took a seat on a squeaky swivel chair behind an aged desk, its surface buried under files. A window loomed behind him—its outer frame draped in spiderwebs. Beyond the glass, the only thing visible was the hospital's tall brick chimney, which rose so high that it disappeared beyond the top frame of the dirty window.

Dr. Chan wore thick black-frame reading glasses like the kind you see in old movies. His black hair was uncombed, and he smelled of cigarettes. Just like the man in the hallway, I couldn't discern the doctor's age, but I guessed late fifties, though something told me he was younger.

He flashed me a smile that never reached his eyes, and it vanished as quickly as it had appeared. "I'm Dr. Chan. Your physician has sent me the details of your file, and she's concerned that you aren't responding to the prescribed antidepressants, even with the two dose increases over the last four months. She's seeking out my professional opinion at this juncture to see how we should proceed with the medication. Going forward, I think we need to bring it up once again, but as you'll be at the higher end of the recommended dose for these types of antidepressants, she has expressed concern about the third increase."

I shifted uneasily in my seat and forced myself to ask, "Will this increase the side effects? I'm already dealing with constipation, constant naps, and I can barely focus on the smallest of tasks."

He leaned back in his chair and spoke through a grin, holding it much too long. "Well, your file says you're no longer feeling constantly depressed, but the panic attacks persist. I think it's worth increasing the dose if it can do away with your anxiety—don't you?"

Something about Dr. Chan just wasn't right. His grin felt like it belonged to someone watching a game they'd already won. He didn't really care if these side effects were making me miserable. He wasn't even pretending to care. Clearly, my doctor had informed him that I reported feeling less depressed, and he was using that as the green light to increase the dose to calm the panic attacks.

"Is there at least some other medication I can try?" My question seemed to tighten his expression, as if I'd crossed a line.

"This is the best medication available for your condition. I wouldn't recommend changing it at this point in the treatment." He shuffled through the papers in his folder, then turned his wrist over to look at his watch. Without looking up, he said, "I see here you've informed your doctor you're seeing a psychologist?"

Trying to disguise the nervousness in my voice, I began to explain, "I haven't started seeing him yet, but my first appointment has been scheduled for the end of this week." My anxiety with this man was taking over. I desperately wanted to leave.

"Is there any way we can give the drugs a little more time at the current dose, before we increase it once more?" I asked in desperation, hoping he would show some sign of understanding. "Constantly feeling miserable from all of the side effects of these drugs is starting to be just as bad as the panic attacks."

He took out a prescription pad and started to write. "You've been on them long enough to see results. If we haven't seen improvement with the panic attacks at this point, it's just not going to happen at the current dose." He spoke flatly, without looking up. "Some patients find that the side effects ease off after a few weeks at the higher dose. I'll need to see you next week to follow up closely on your new regimen."

He tore the sheet free from the pad and slid it across the desk through the only available free space between the stacks of files. The yellow folder tabs were lined with faceless names, each marked with a bold red number. I stared at them—case after case of people in distress, their suffering catalogued, contained, and now at the mercy of the man sitting in front of me.

"You can go downstairs to the hospital pharmacy to have it filled. If you haven't already taken today's pill, you can start the new prescription right away. Follow the signs from the elevator on the ground floor—you'll find it." He stood up, walked to the door, and told me to call the same number I used before to arrange my follow up appointment.

I stepped out of his office feeling alone and hopeless. I made my way down the hall. This just didn't feel right. I was feeling more desperate than ever as I stepped onto the elevator and made my way down to the pharmacy.

Before arriving on the main floor, the door opened and a very old woman lying on a hospital bed was wheeled on by an orderly. There were tubes in her arms and an oxygen mask covered most of her face. Her arms were out on top of the blanket that covered the rest of her body. She was practically skin and bones and her eyes—open, grey, and sunken deep into her eye sockets. She, as well, stared into the darkness.

I tried not to stare, but my eyes kept finding their way back to her. The woman looked ever so slightly in my direction, and our eyes met. I was startled; I hadn't expected her attention. A faint but unmistakable smile formed beneath the oxygen mask. Her eyes went clearer, and a glow began to replace the darkness that had previously been there. I smiled back, then glanced at the orderly. He took no notice of our exchange, his gaze fixed on the elevator floor numbers above the door.

We reached the ground floor. I stepped off, turning, watching the elevator door close. The old woman and her attendant continued the descent to the lower levels of the hospital. Before the doors had completely closed, I could see the brightness in her eyes and the smile that still remained.

I followed the signs for the pharmacy which were clearly indicated and led me directly there. I waited in the line watching the pharmacists and assistants busily moving about, attending to the many customers ahead of me. The prescription was prepared quickly, and the pharmacist came over to speak with me. She wanted to make sure I had a follow-up appointment with Dr. Chan. "These are rather strong, and you'll need to be closely monitored for side effects," she said, with clear concern on her face.

I assured her that it would be arranged as soon as I got home. She nodded and dropped the small pill bottle into a white paper bag that was far too big for the medication. I reached in and removed the bottle, slipping it into my pocket. I thanked her and paid for the prescription.

It was close to noon when I left the hospital. A steady drizzle was falling, and the air still carried a winter chill. I was desperate to be outside. Despite the weather, I decided to walk home.

The third week of spring and the sun hadn't shown itself in days. I pulled the collar of my jacket close around my neck, folded my arms across my chest, and headed toward home. All I felt was fear and misery. The rain slowly soaked into my windbreaker, and my pants from the knee down were drenched, but I didn't care.

I thought about the old woman in the elevator—how fragile she had looked. What does it feel like to be at the end of your days, when change is no longer possible? To be left with the voice of self-scrutiny, praising or condemning you for the life you lived. I was already feeling so much regret. So much defeat. Were these drugs going to dull every remaining chance at joy? How would I tolerate yet another increase?

My mind was a torrent of questions without answers, each one pulling me deeper into the dark.

The streets were quiet, a light fog settling over them. The heavy clouds made it feel more like dusk than afternoon. I pulled the pill bottle from my pocket and looked at its contents. Such tiny tablets. How could something so small have such a massive grip on my life? The psychiatrist hadn't asked a single personal question. Weren't they supposed to ask about your childhood or something?

I didn't see how the medication was supposed to change anything. Sure, the depression felt less sharp, but the negative thoughts were louder, more invasive. The pills seemed to hold me in an in-between world—where nothing was good, nothing was bad. Just…nothing. A liminal state.

Reminders all around me of the life I could live, but no will to reach for it. Just the numbness.

There was still one choice I could make. I shook the bottle and listened to the pills rattle. Gripping it tight—anger surging—I hurled it into a nearby garbage bin. "To hell with this," I muttered under my breath.

Almost instantly, regret hit. The self-doubt was already clawing its way in. I wasn't the kind of person to make rash decisions, said the voice inside—my inner judge, always waiting. But deeper down, I knew this was what I had to do.

I kept walking. My doctor's warning echoed in my mind—come off the medication slowly or risk increased side effects. I pushed the thought away, cursing myself for always doubting, always second-guessing. I wiped the rain from my face. What did it matter? I was going to feel like a zombie either way.

I looked up. The drizzle struck my face like needles. Then came the tears—frustration, helplessness, dependence: on pills, on doctors, on psychiatrists. There was no peace from the storm in my brain, and no one seemed to know how to help. I don't know who I was talking to, but I whispered into the rain, "please help me. My life feels like it's over—please show me a way to find meaning again. I haven't given up. But I need a sign. Something— or someone—to help me find my way back."

The rain fell harder. I walked on, drenched and indifferent. The dark loneliness closed in, wrapping around me like a second skin. Panic stirred beneath it. The sadness was heavier, swallowing the surge of anxiety—but the fear pressed harder still. There was the desire to run. I couldn't. There was nowhere left to go.

A Leap of Faith

The rain stopped and warm rays of sun cut through the few remaining scattered clouds. I tried taking a few deep breaths to calm myself down. Shallow as they were, they relieved some tightness from my chest. I looked up to allow the warmth to touch my face, and the welcome heat helped to calm my shivers.

The bright sun glared off the surrounding windows, making me squint. Through the shimmer, I spotted a sign in an upper-floor window of a plain grey apartment building across the street. It read, Bliss Centre, 3rd floor.

Without a second thought, I ran across the street and entered the foyer of the building where the sign was displayed. There was a board indicating the names and apartments of its occupants, with an intercom to access the main entrance. I rang the number for the Bliss Centre, praying someone would answer, as my thoughts of despair continued to invade, removing any glimpse of a break from the emptiness I was feeling. My breathing had returned to feeling restricted and short.

A soft, yet deep and calm voice came over the intercom asking who was there. I tried to answer in a tone that hid my desperation and told the man I was seeking information about the Bliss Centre. He said to come up, and the buzzer sounded, releasing the door.

The elevator was old, dimly lit, rickety, and slow, which wasn't helping my nerves—and had me on the edge of feeling suffocated. There was a mirror covering the wall to the right of the door. My face in its reflection was pale, my eyes heavy with dark circles. The poor lighting reflected what almost looked like a much older man. It was a broken version of a person I could no longer recognize—the ravages of an overactive mind. The door finally opened on the third floor, and as I stepped off, I was met with the scent of incense.

It was a long corridor, as dimly lit as the elevator, with an old but clean green carpeted floor. At the very end of the hallway, I could see a sign on a door indicating the Bliss Centre. All the doors were grey, each with black apartment number plates on the centre, just above the peephole. As I walked past, I caught the sound of ordinary life spilling through each door: a baby crying while a sweet voice sang a lullaby in a language I didn't recognize, a vacuum cleaner humming, the laughter of a woman, a television game show on far too loud, and a telephone ringing. Beneath it all, the scent of incense was pulling me forward—warm, growing stronger with each step. I'd walked past this building a hundred times, never once noticing it. Yet now, each step felt purposeful, necessary—like I was supposed to be here.

I stopped at door 300. My breath was shallow. Panic still hovered at the edges of my chest, but something deeper was present too—a silence in my mind, a stillness beneath the anxiety.

Feeling awkward and nervous, I stood in the dim hallway trying to compose myself. All I had left was hope that whatever awaited me behind this door was going to be my way forward, even without knowing who was there or what they offered. Surely, anything claiming to be a Bliss Centre must offer something that could even partially liberate a troubled mind.

I raised my hand and tapped gently.

Footsteps approached from the other side. When the door opened, I was met by a small Indian man, whose deep brown eyes instantly held me in a state of calm.

He was maybe five-foot five, broad-chested with strong shoulders that tapered into a slim waist. His dark skin was weathered but vibrant, and his thick arms spoke of a life shaped by physical discipline.

19

He wore white from head to toe—a short-sleeve collared shirt, matching track pants, pristine white socks, and no shoes.

Without a word, he pressed his palms together and gave a slight bow. Then, with an open hand and a gentle nod, he invited me in.

The smell of incense was immediate—this was the source. I stepped inside, and he closed the door behind me, the hallway and the outside world felt as though they had vanished. Without being told, I removed my shoes.

He smiled warmly and asked how he could help me. The moment felt so deeply meaningful, even though there had been no significant exchange. I almost fell to my knees, feeling that I had reached a distant shore and was finally safe. But I held myself upright and said the only thing I could think of:

"I saw the sign…and I don't know why, but I felt drawn here. What is the Bliss Centre?"

He didn't answer. Instead, he turned silently and led me down the hall. What opened before me was not an apartment—it was a temple. The room was flooded with color. There was no furniture, only red and gold pillows laid about the floor. In each corner, lush palms rose from ceramic pots, their fronds dancing gently in the breeze of a ceiling fan. A woven rug filled the floor—on it, a scene depicting warriors with bows and arrows riding chariots into what gave the impression of a quiet battle. Somehow the scene, though filled with tension, radiated serenity.

The walls were draped in tapestries: herons under crescent moons, ancient symbols I couldn't read, and weavings that pulsed softly with the light. At the far end stood a wooden statue, about four feet tall—half-man, half-elephant, adorned in carved jewelry and crowned with an ornate headdress. At its feet, a single incense stick burned in a clay dish, casting a thin spiral of smoke toward the ceiling like a thread to another world.

Then something happened. The tightness in my chest lessened, my shoulders dropped, and I could feel my heartbeat slow. I felt peaceful, safe, maybe even seen.

He sat cross-legged on one of the pillows and motioned for me to do the same. I tried—awkwardly, uncomfortably—wrapping my arms around my legs to stay upright. I must've looked like a wounded bird trying to fold itself into stillness. Finally, I settled, then breathed. When I looked up at the wise Indian man, he sat patiently—eyes steady, breath calm. He was waiting for me.

His gaze softened further, and he answered my question, with presence and connection.

"Welcome to the Bliss Centre…and my home," he said in a low resonant, voice. "My name is Guruji Mandeep. People simply call me Guruji."

He paused and breathed deeply, almost like he didn't want to rush the introduction and wanted to allow silence to find a place in the exchange.

"We can speak about what we do here in a moment. But first…more importantly…I want to know: how are you, truly? You seem to be carrying weight. Your breath is unsettled, and your eyes hold the kind of sadness born of many years past. I sense you're not just struggling…you're running."

How could he see so clearly? His words weren't guesses—they felt spoken by someone who had seen this before. I thought I'd hidden it well, the way I always did. But I suddenly recalled the elevator mirror—that disheveled figure staring back. Maybe I hadn't hidden anything at all. There was no point pretending. Not here. Not with this man.

I looked up, and he met my eyes. His gaze wasn't probing or intense—it was calm, seeing. His presence beckoned honesty. I felt no judgment in him, only a kind presence rooted in something deeper than what we are accustomed to. Something told me this man had sat with pain before. Not just his own—but the kind that lingers in others, year after year, waiting to be called out, waiting to be named.

"My name is Rohan," I said, trying to steady my voice. "Great to meet you, uh…Mr. Guruji?"

His smile widened slightly, amused but not mocking. "It's just Guruji," he said gently.

"Right," I replied, stumbling. "Sorry. I just…it doesn't feel respectful to use someone's first name like that."

He read the discomfort on my face, and with the ease of someone used to softening tension, explained: "In Sanskrit, Guruji means teacher. Or guide. It's not a name—it's a relationship."

That settled something in me. "Well, it's an honour to meet you…Guruji."

He tilted his head. "It's curious you have the name Rohan," he said. "In our culture, Rohan means ascending—growth, elevation. A name of journey."

I let out a half-chuckle. "That's funny. My mom told me it's Irish. Usually spelled Rowan, but she liked the 'h'. Said it means red or rusty…and something else…I don't remember." I trailed off. His meaning felt mythic; mine felt mundane. A part of me wanted to trade stories and become the Rohan of journey.

Guruji smiled again. "A fine name in any tongue," he said. "Names arrive before we understand them. Now…" his voice dropped to something quieter, not softer. "Tell me, what is it that troubles you?"

We hadn't yet talked about his services, fees, or even what this place really was. I felt awkward taking up his time like this, but I pressed on.

I glanced down at the woven battle scene beneath us, and when I looked up again, the words just came out.

"I feel like I'm falling apart," I said. "I think I'm losing my mind. Some days I feel okay…like I'm getting better. But then—out of nowhere— this surge hits me. Panic. Like I'm slipping into a dark pit, and I can't stop it. It's like being buried alive. My thoughts race, I can't breathe, and I just…disappear." The words hung in the air. They were called out.

I'd always avoided describing that feeling out loud—afraid it would make it more real. But here, in this strange and sacred place, the words didn't feel dangerous. They felt true. It was as if speaking them aloud began to loosen their grip.

"I don't know what you do here," I said quietly. "But I'm desperate. I need help."

I shifted my weight uncomfortably, leaning into my right hip to try and ease the ache. My back was on fire. My legs had gone numb, feet tingling with pins and needles. I couldn't imagine sitting here much longer in this position. Yet across from me, Guruji hadn't moved an inch—still as stone. Effortless. Rooted. He watched me not as a therapist or doctor, but as something…older. Deeper.

He nodded slightly, closing his eyes…and drew in a deep breath. So deep his belly and rib cage seemed to expand to twice their size as they filled with air. Then slowly, he exhaled—a long, controlled release that sounded like air escaping a rubber raft. I'm sure my mouth was wide open as I stared in wonder.

Guruji then opened his eyes and spoke with calm certainty.

"Young man, you are simply out of balance," he said, as if stating a fact of nature. "Your body, your mind, your spirit—they are misaligned. Like a wheel with one broken spoke, you cannot move forward without stumbling. When these three fall out of harmony, the body weakens, the mind becomes clouded, and the spirit…forgets how to grow. And without growth, there is suffering. Cycles repeat. Clarity vanishes. Peace flees."

It sounded so simple when he said it. Like balance was just something I'd misplaced. But to me, it felt impossible—like being handed a map with no roads indicated, but told to find a destination. "I beg your pardon, Guruji," I said, shifting again to relieve the fire in my back. "I'm not sure I understand. Out of balance? Spirit and body not working together? I wouldn't even know where to begin fixing that. All I know is…I want peace."

I took a breath—shallow, shaky—and immediately felt ashamed of it, in comparison to his.

"Peace." Guruji said, pausing and looking deep into my eyes. "Peace is a worthy longing. But peace is not a gift that descends upon the unready. It is earned through small actions—simple but necessary steps. To walk the path of peace, one must cultivate discipline in three directions—body, mind, and spirit—and not treat any one as less important."

He leaned in slightly, not abruptly, but quietly. "There is a recipe. And I will share it with you. But you must be willing to act—patiently, and without expectation."

He held my gaze and said the words I most needed to hear: "I can help you."

It didn't feel like an offer. It felt like a promise. It had been less than fifteen minutes since I stepped through his door, and yet…some part of me already trusted this man, and knew he could help me.

Still, reality tapped on my shoulder. I needed to know—could I even afford sessions with Guruji? Could I sustain the time I needed to work with him. I was sure this would take time.

"I'd love to do this work with you," I said, hesitating, not wanting to interrupt the moment. "But…how do I make appointments with you? And what are your fees?"

He replied in a soft and almost offhand tone, "You may put whatever payment per session you are able to afford in a sealed envelope, and place it at the feet of Lord Ganesha at the end of each meeting." His hand moved in a slow gesture toward the wooden statue of the half- man, half-elephant, still crowned in incense smoke.

My mind immediately scrambled: What is the value of these sessions? How am I supposed to figure out what is acceptable? What if I insult him and give too little?

He interrupted my thoughts and explained, "For now we must start with something simple, and do not mistake simple for small. Just one simple action step—if done with intention—is all it takes to open the direction of your path towards peace and a more meaningful life."

I shifted again. Pins and needles surged through my legs, and my spine pulsed with sharp, urgent pain. As hopeful as I was, I couldn't imagine how I was supposed to pursue peace—or focus on any *steps*—when my entire body was screaming in protest.

Guruji inhaled slowly, his belly and chest rising once more with that same effortless grace.

27

When he exhaled, he spoke quietly, like revealing something sacred. "The first ingredient in the recipe for peace," he said, "is harmony in the body. When your physical form is in pain, out of rhythm, or neglected…peace cannot anchor itself. Your breath will become tight, your thoughts scatter, and you will not be able to see your path with clarity—the spirit then becomes restless."

His eyes didn't move from mine. He continued, "Right now, you are unable to sit without pain—but that can change. Your muscles, joints, blood flow, lungs, and brain…all of these must learn to move together—in balance, in rhythm. We each have our own limits, and perfection is never the goal. What matters is that you explore to the edge of your own capacity. To take care of your body is to show yourself love."

He folded his hands gently on his lap, then continued. "You do not need to become an athlete or pursue intense exercise. That is not the point. The point is structure, breath, and attention. A little effort each day, given consistently, can return you to harmony with your physical self. When we hurt, we cannot focus on healing—only on surviving. But when we treat our body with care, even its imperfections become part of the path."

I was struck by how calm his words made me feel, even as my body throbbed.

Then, with sudden weight in his voice, he added: "Promise yourself this: never look to the path of another. It is not yours to walk. Envy, comparison—these are illusions that steal your energy. You must walk *your* path. No one else can."

He breathed in again—as he had before. Expanding and growing.

"Soon," he said, "I will teach you disciplines that unite the parts of you that feel broken—body, mind, and spirit. This is my way, the way I was taught. You may discover other practices along your journey. There are many ways to make us whole—but each path must be walked with courage. We cannot recoil the moment we encounter conflict. For now, your task is simple: Three times per day, sit in this position for fifteen minutes. Breathe. Breathe deeply. Inhale life. Oxygen is not just air—it is energy, it is vision. Without breath, your path remains hidden."

His words, though incredibly inspiring; I was struggling to see how I could ever find the harmony he described. I was feeling so broken. I hadn't even lasted five minutes in this position—how would I survive fifteen? My back felt like an unbendable slab of stone. My feet were a pincushion, and I was convinced I'd need surgery just to stand up again. Meanwhile, Guruji sat like a mountain—unmoving, undisturbed.

"Now," he said, adjusting his posture—somehow, even taller than before, "we begin your first lesson."

His voice lowered, and something in the air around us shifted—as though the room itself were preparing for what was next.

"Breathing," he said, "should not live in the chest—that is where shallow fears hide. Deep breath begins in the belly. When you inhale, the belly expands first…then the chest. In that order. The shoulders remain still, relaxed—they are not there to assist breathing."

He paused, watching my face, letting the words sink in.

"This," he said, "is how we begin."

I tried to sit taller in the newly learned cross-legged position, but the ache in my lower back made it unbelievably difficult. No matter how I shifted, I couldn't find stillness—only stiffness and sharp jolts of pain. Guruji, of course, noticed.

"Close your eyes," he said gently. "And listen to my breath."

Before I closed my eyes, I witnessed Guruji rubbing his hands together briskly—as if waking them up—and then a subtle stillness, as he brought them together, in the form of cupping an invisible ball. I closed my eyes.

His rhythmic breathing filled the room. Deep, slow, unwavering. "Inhale with me," he said, his voice a low hum. "Feel the breath enter your belly. Let it fill you with healing. As you exhale…release the pain. Let it flow from your body like smoke."

Try as I might, the pain kept flaring. My hips screamed. My spine throbbed. My legs were numb. Still…something happened.

The deeper I breathed, the more something else began to stir. A sudden warmth bloomed through my back—like a firm hand pressing gently between my shoulder blades, guiding me upright. The pain didn't vanish, but it softened. Then came a sensation in my neck—a lengthening, as if an invisible thread were lifting me toward the ceiling. My spine straightened without effort. My body relaxed, opened.

I kept my eyes closed, trying not to question it. Weightlessness washed over me. My thoughts dimmed. My anxiety, for a moment, dissolved like fog lifting under the morning sun. And then came something stranger—a sensation of emptiness moving through me. But it wasn't frightening. Not at first. It was…spacious. Free. Like I'd set down a heavy pack I didn't know I was carrying.

As I drifted further inward, a sliver of fear broke through. What was it? What was happening to me? A dark ripple stirred at the edges of my mind—a whisper of that familiar abyss. I panicked. Afraid I might lose myself; I opened my eyes.

There sat Guruji—exactly as before. Eyes closed. Breathing softly. His palms still hovering around the invisible orb of energy.

I felt confused—had he done something? I couldn't describe it, there was a feeling, the space between us palpable…like something happened through him and touched me.

Whatever it was, it vanished. In an instant— and pain came flooding back into my body like a crashing wave. Once again, the seated posture became impossible to hold.

Guruji opened his eyes slowly. I stared at him, unsure of what to say. Did he know what just happened? Did *anything* happen? Or had I imagined the whole thing?

I hesitated, caught between awe and confusion, then finally muttered, "…that was incredible."

I waited, half-hoping he would acknowledge it. Validate what just happened. To my surprise, he said nothing. He just looked at me— the faintest knowing glimmer in his eyes.

"You will practice your sitting and breathing exercise," Guruji said, "for the next four days before we meet again."

His voice had settled into that calm cadence that made everything feel just right.

"We must always prepare for any great journey...but too often, we confuse preparation for movement, and never truly begin. It is the action steps—however small—that illuminate the road ahead. If your intentions are clear, and you do the work with sincerity, you will begin to notice signs—everywhere. They will whisper to you: 'You are on the right path.' And your path," he added, "is the one that leads to peace."

We arranged the day and time for our next meeting. I told him I would bring payment for both today and the next session when I saw him in four days.

He placed a warm hand on my shoulder and smiled, "That would be just fine," he said. "But remember—as we agreed—place only what you are able to give, in a sealed envelope. Leave it at the feet of Lord Ganesha. This is the last we will speak of payment."

His tone was final, but not cold—more like a closing ritual, not a dismissal, not making it seem unimportant.

He walked me to the door, and as I stepped out, he pressed his palms together and offered a soft bow—the same gesture as when I arrived. I clumsily mirrored him, feeling awkward but trying my best to show respect.

The hallway was still now—silent. No crying babies, no humming vacuums, no game shows or laughter. Only the steady thump of my heartbeat as I walked back toward the elevator.

What just happened in there? I didn't have a name for the sensation I had experienced. That warmth. That straightening of my back. The strange emptiness that had filled me with something like peace—then vanished when I opened my eyes. The dark shadow—it was there too.

I should have asked Guruji what this experience was. I'd been too concerned about looking foolish. Whatever it was, I wouldn't forget it—not for a long time, maybe never.

The silence was deafening.

The Willow

As I stepped out of the apartment building, thin ribbons of sunlight broke through the scattered clouds, carrying with them, warmth and muted radiance. The grey sky had nearly cleared, and the air itself seemed to shift—warmer now, gentler. Everything around me felt subtly…changed. Not in any way you could point to, not visibly or obviously, but undeniably so. Maybe it was the lingering afterglow of my time with Guruji—but even that explanation felt incomplete. There was a softness in me now, a quiet spaciousness I hadn't ever felt.

It was only then that I noticed my clothes were still damp from the rain, clinging faintly to my skin. I had become oblivious to it while I was with Guruji. The drying rays of the sun felt good.

On my way home, I felt a pull— not a plan, but a quiet nudge from somewhere beneath thought—and found myself turning into the majestic city park. But to call it a park felt small. It was a sanctuary: a wide expanse of towering maples, ash, oak, and elm—some so ancient, they seemed to hold time itself in their branches—nature's own cathedral. Even on the hottest days, the park held its own cool shade. The trees didn't just block the sun—they transformed it, spilling gold and green light, that fell softly on the ground below.

The park had always called to me. Often in passing, I'd feel it—a whisper to slow down, step inside, listen. But like most whispers, I'd learned to tune it out. Today, I didn't.

I followed the stone path inward—a trail pressed flat and solid from decades of footsteps, by people seeking refuge from the noise. The crushed gravel offered a subtle, satisfying crunch beneath me—a welcome shift from the unyielding hardness of the city sidewalk.

It was spring, and everywhere, life was pressing up from the ground—daffodils and tulips in soft reds and sunny yellows, curling open toward the light. The grass was vivid from weeks of rain, and golden dandelions spotted the hills—providing first nectar of the season for the pollinators.

Each step carried me further from the city. The hum of traffic thinned, then vanished. The skyline disappeared behind the trees. Even the air changed—quieter, touched with the scent of earth and leaves. From inside the park, it was hard to believe the city still existed at all.

I remembered coming here as a boy—picnics, games, sunburns. Faded memories now, but still clear enough to feel. Those were the days when mom would make those tiny egg salad sandwiches on soft dinner rolls. I'd beg her to make them for lunches at home, but she'd just smile and say, *"then they wouldn't be as special on a picnic."* I grinned at the thought. She was right.

Suddenly, I was enveloped by the sounds of birdsong—hundreds of melodies weaving together in the canopy above. The rustling of leaves in the soft breeze had come to replace the distant drone of city traffic, as if the very air had turned a page.

At the heart of the park lay a broad, glimmering pond—a natural basin that felt untouched, almost sacred. A ring of large and small boulders traced its shoreline, like ancient guardians, giving the impression that the water belonged to a forgotten forest, far from the city's reach.

Last summer's water grasses and bulrushes stood dry and brittle—faded—as a remaining memory of a season past. Between their stalks, small chickadees and sparrows landed briefly, tilting the fragile reeds toward the shimmering water's surface. Tiny green shoots had begun to emerge, nudging their way up through the damp earth, hinting at the new life that spring promised.

Dragonflies, skimmed across the water in flickering bursts—their wings barely brushing the surface, leaving behind circles that rippled gently outward.

I stood and breathed it all in. For the first time in what felt like forever, something loosened in me. Peace—faint, unfamiliar, but unmistakably glimmering beneath the surface of my thoughts.

Then I saw it.

Across the pond, on the far bank, stood a willow tree—the willow. Its silvery leaves shimmered in the breeze, cascading like a waterfall of green light that gently touched the still surface of the pond. Each gust sent the branches swaying in slow, deliberate rhythms—almost hypnotizing.

There was no rush. The park was nearly empty, so I followed the call of the willow. As I walked the gravel path toward it, a slow-moving figure emerged from a bend in the path ahead. A middle-aged Asian man, came trotting along at perhaps the gentlest jogging pace I'd ever seen. He wore a light grey cotton tracksuit and impossibly white running shoes. His posture was tall and upright, his expression serene—smiling not just with his eyes but his whole being. The happiest runner I'd ever seen.

As we passed one another, I offered, "It certainly turned out to be a wonderful day for a jog."

He didn't need to stop—his pace was practically a walking meditation.

"Niko niko," he said with a cheerful bow of the head.

Then, in broken but deliberate English, he said, "Niko niko—slow running in Japan. Slow…so I can talk. Slow…so I can breathe deeply. And especially slow…so I can smile." He tapped his temple gently, "slow for a happy mind," he added.

We shared a heartfelt laugh. With a wave over his shoulder, he carried on, disappearing into the trees, with the same unhurried grace. His footsteps, no more than a whisper against the gravel.

"Slow for a happy mind," I repeated silently. I liked that.

I turned back toward the willow. Even though the sun was soft and the air cool, the tree's canopy called to me—not just for its shade, but for something deeper. It felt like shelter.

I settled with my back supported against the great trunk, and faced the sparkling pond. Though I had only just left Guruji's centre, I wanted to practice the breathing and posture exercises while they were still fresh in my mind. Part of me was simply curious—curious to see if I could summon that same liberating sensation I'd felt with him, that fleeting but powerful clarity brought on by breath.

With my back against the tree, the cross-legged position came easier. The stabbing sensation in my spine was gone, and I could finally breathe with some comfort. I closed my eyes and began inhaling slowly through my nose, letting my belly fill with air, then expanding my chest. Shoulders down, neck relaxed—I exhaled in a slow, controlled stream, just as Guruji had instructed. I imagined drawing in the healing energy of oxygen and exhaling pain, sickness, and tension.

My body began to straighten. My hips softened. The wind brushed the willow's leaves above, their rustle a calming breath over the pond. That familiar emptiness returned—at first a gentle presence, almost welcoming, but it shifted quickly.

A shadow stirred. Not one I could see, but one I could feel—reaching, pulling, drawing me toward that place where all sense of self unravels. A void. A vacuum of thought. A darkness so deep it dissolved everything into shapeless black. Terror seized me.

My eyes flew open, and I lurched to my feet, yet the abyss clung to me. I was partly back in my body, but not all the way—something of me still adrift in that darkness. Panic flared like fire beneath my skin, but I gripped at what I could—the pond, the trees, the willow, Guruji. *I'm not alone anymore,* I told myself. I have a way forward.

Bit by bit, the fear loosened its grip. My breath was still broken, my body trembling from head to toe—then, a sudden flash: the middle-aged Japanese man jogging past, his wide smile beaming as he tapped his temple and said, *"Especially slow for happy thoughts."*

Somewhere deep inside, I felt the pull to move. Not run away—that never worked—but to move with something. To change the rhythm. To challenge the fear.

I was tired of living in fear, worn thin by the weight of suffocating panic. But maybe now, I could test it. I would run. This time I wouldn't be paralyzed with fear, but push myself into motion— and then maybe, just maybe, it would prove this fear didn't own me.

I'd worn my old sneakers to the appointment. They weren't perfect—they weren't pristine—but they'd do. I hadn't run in over a year, but I set off at a slow, steady pace. *Niko niko,* I thought—just like the man said. Slow enough to breathe deeply. Slow enough to smile. Fast enough to prove the shadow won't stop me.

After about fifteen minutes, I was only mildly out of breath. My lungs pushed hard, but there was no panic, no hint of suffocation. Somewhere around the twenty-five-minute mark, it struck me—the panic I'd felt earlier in the park had vanished completely.

41

I still had another fifteen minutes before I'd reach home, but I decided to take a detour and keep running. Just a little longer.

The sun was beginning to set behind the mountain west of the city. I found myself on a stretch of open road, as if the universe had cleared a path for me to run straight into the sky—a glorious canvas of orange and pink spilling across the horizon.

I remembered Guruji's instructions and breathed deep into my belly, letting the breath rise into my chest. I pictured the Japanese man again—smiling, light, alive—and kept my shoulders down, my neck relaxed, my posture tall. I ran with a slight forward lean, landing on the balls of my feet, and for the first time in months, I felt my body was my friend.

The cool spring evening had been transformed into a palette of radiant color. As the sun slipped behind the mountain, it washed the entire city in a golden-orange glow. I eased my pace, recalling the words—*niko niko.* I'd been pushing too hard, chasing the last light, and gently pulled myself back to ease.

I stopped running about a block from my house and walked the remaining distance. My mind was clear. My body felt awake.

And I thought to myself…Tomorrow would be a good day.

The Old Woman

The treasure we seek requires no lengthy expedition, no expensive equipment, no superior aptitude or special company. All we lack is the willingness to imagine that we already have everything we need. The only thing missing is our consent to be where we are.

—Pema Chodron

The next morning, I awoke feeling well-rested. I slept more peacefully than I had in ages. I must have been exhausted; I couldn't even remember getting into bed. Sometimes the antidepressants left me disoriented, like I'd been drinking, warping my sense of time. I felt slightly dizzy, and the brain fog was thick, but I knew these side effects well—and was relieved they were no worse than usual.

My schedule was wide open; I had nothing planned for the day—and wouldn't for weeks. Between jobs, with four weeks until I started with my new employer, time had opened up in a way I wasn't used to. I'd grown accustomed to life being perpetually scheduled, with barely any space to just be. Even my so-called free time had been filled with reservations, appointments, people to meet—rarely anything spontaneous. Now I was being forced to slow down, and it didn't feel good. Unstructured days left too much room to think—about how lost I felt, and how far my life seemed from the one I'd imagined.

I was looking forward to the new role—being around people again. I missed most of my former colleagues. With few close friendships of my own, the people I worked with had become a kind of stand-in for connection. They'd promised to keep in touch, but life had a way of rearranging priorities—not from malice, but from the pull of whatever feels most urgent in the moment.

A genuine smile rose as I thought of Guruji. Four weeks lay ahead—four weeks to work with him, to see if there was a chance at finding peace, at building something deeper than mere survival.

I had my morning coffee and a quick bite for breakfast. The forecast promised a full day of sunshine, and I wanted to get to the park first thing.

My legs were feeling sore, and the center of my back ached as if I'd spent the day doing heavy lifting. Could all this soreness be from just sitting straight and breathing deeply? Maybe some of it was from yesterday's run, too. Either way, I was looking forward to getting my body moving again this evening.

Instead of taking the bus, I rode my bike to the park. It would cut down on travel time, give me some early morning exercise, and still leave room for a few errands before tonight's run. I slipped a water bottle and some snacks into my backpack, and I was on my way.

The streets were quiet, the city only just beginning to stir. I hadn't taken my bike out in ages, and I'd forgotten how much I enjoyed it. Biking, walking, jogging—they always made me feel more connected to everything around me. There's something about moving slowly—closer to the earth, closer to ourselves. From inside a car or bus, the world passes in a blur. But at the pace of breath and heartbeat, the ordinary begins to speak.

Walking, especially seemed to grant permission to pause, observe, and imagine. It was as if all five senses were finally given their rightful time. Maybe that's what the Japanese man meant by *niko niko*—not just slow running, but the joy of moving gently enough to notice the beauty hiding in plain sight. What I felt yesterday wasn't the old familiar runner's high. It was something deeper: a quiet aliveness that reached past endorphins and touched something more essential.

I stopped at a red light and noticed an old woman I'd seen before, carefully placing books out on display in front of her tiny bookstore. The building was easy to overlook—a squat, weathered stone-and-wood cottage pressed between two sleek modern brownstones, like a forgotten relic from another century. It had a slanted shingled roof, ivy cascading from flower boxes beneath the windows, and a crooked little chimney that looked like it belonged in a storybook.

In the window, dreamcatchers swayed gently, and crystals caught the rising sun. I'd passed it so many times before, always dismissing it as quirky or out of place. But today something felt different. The store, the woman—they felt like they had been waiting for me.

She looked up from her stand and smiled warmly. Her eyes were light, almost translucent blue, and seemed to hold a hundred untold stories. Her skin was deep and weathered, her white-silver hair braided loosely, with streaks of dark still winding through. She wore a long, flowing dress patterned with birds and butterflies—like a tapestry of nature.

"Go on in, take a look," she said, her accent lilting with something tropical, something sun-soaked and distant. "I'll be right here if you need anything."

I leaned my bike gently against the shop wall and stepped inside. Immediately, I was met with the soothing scent of incense. It wasn't overpowering—just enough to make the air feel softened, like something sacred lived here.

I poked my head back out the door. "What's that smell? It's beautiful."

"Sandalwood," she said, smiling, as she approached, then leaned through the doorway and drew in a slow deep breath. "My favorite—good for healing, peace, and lifting the spirit."

"I'll definitely take a box," I said, smiling back. "I think I need a bit of all three." I meant it more than she could have known.

"Take your time," she said, before vanishing back into the shop's outer world.

Inside, old books leaned into each other on aged wooden shelves, each one seemingly whispering to be chosen. It was the sort of place that required patience—like time moved differently inside, and only those who lingered could find what they were meant to.

As I wandered the aisles, the wooden floor creaked beneath my feet, the dusty scent of pages mingling with sandalwood. It conjured the feeling that I'd slipped into some other space—not quite past, not quite future. The store was so silent it made you want to whisper. I had no idea what I was looking for, but somehow, I felt like something here was looking for me.

The woman returned, placing her emptied book box on the floor by one of the bookcases. "Finding everything you're looking for?" she asked with a smile.

"I certainly am," I replied.

"What brought you into my shop today?" she asked, with a knowing grin. "I've seen you pass by many times—never so much as a glance through the window." Then she laughed, a warm, melodic sound, eyes twinkling with a teasing sweetness.

I chuckled, a bit shy. "To be honest, since yesterday everything around me just seems different…I'm noticing things. I don't know how to explain it."

The old woman nodded gently and stepped closer, her gaze scanning me slowly from head to toe, as though she were reading something beneath the surface—something I myself hadn't quite found the words for.

"Something in your world has shifted," she murmured, her voice carrying the weight of knowing. "The stirring of your spirit has begun. Tell me—has the light around you changed? I see shadows moving where they didn't dwell before."

There was something disarming about her presence—kind, grounded, with a quiet power that made me want to confide in her. But her question…it landed like an arrow. For a moment, I wondered if she could see something in me no one else ever had.

"Shadows?" I echoed, my voice lower than I expected. "Yeah…I suppose you could say shadows have been moving lately." I gave a small uneasy chuckle. "Most of my life has felt like shadows moving. But definitely, more so these days."

I cleared my throat. "Yesterday was… rough. I really needed help—maybe even hoping for a miracle. I called out to…I don't know who or what. My voice felt lost, carried off in the rain. Then I saw a sign for the Bliss Centre on the third floor of a building up the street from here. I went in, met a man named Guruji and…" I shook my head, still unsure how to put the words. "He helped me believe I can get better. There was a calm around him…I had a strange experience there."

I paused, choosing the words carefully.

"When I left, something had shifted in me, even if I couldn't name it. On the way home, I stopped at the city park. I always want to stop, and take it in, but I'm usually too caught up in getting somewhere. There's this incredible willow by the pond. I sat under it, and—for the first time in

49

forever—I could really see the beauty that had been there all along, right under my nose. Something happened inside me. Maybe one day I'll know how to put it into words."

Her smile deepened, and her eyes glistened.

"Isn't it always the way? We often ask ourselves why we didn't do something sooner. Many of the greatest changes in our life aren't from things that happen outside of us; real change happens when we change the way we look at things. The joy, the meaning—it's already around us."

She paused and placed her hand over her heart. "My mother used to say that when those inner shifts begin, life starts showing us the next steps. We begin to notice what she called meaningful coincidences."

What she said struck deep. I'd never quite thought of life that way before.

"That's what Guruji told me," I said.. "If your intention is clear and you do the work, the signs will appear everywhere—confirming that you're on the path."

She placed a hand on my shoulder, her touch warm and grounding. "This Guruji sounds like a wise man. He came into your life right when you were ready to receive him."

"You're pretty wise yourself," I said with a smile, placing the incense on the counter. "How much do I owe you?"

"Just an even five dollars," she replied, her smile unfading.

I handed her the bill, thanked her sincerely, and promised I'd be back soon.

As I stepped outside, climbed onto my bike, and pedaled toward the park, her words echoed in my mind—*something in your world has shifted.* What exactly had she seen in me?

The Heron and the Fish

It took only fifteen minutes to reach the park. As I followed the gravel path, the same sense of calm that had found me yesterday returned, washing over me once more. The sound of the crunching stones beneath my tires was almost hypnotic—steady, familiar, grounding.

As I reached the heart of the park, a breeze carried the fresh earthy-sweet scent of the pond to meet me. Cresting the hill, I saw it—the old willow, radiant in the morning light. Its long green arms reached out over the shimmering water, a guardian keeping watching over the stillness.

I walked my bike the rest of the way down and laid it softly on the grass near the willow's roots. The early spring sun hung low on the horizon, sending golden beams slicing through the tall trees, casting long, delicate shadows. Above, the canopy was alive with birdsong, a chorus of sound that brought an immediate smile to my face.

Where sunlight touched the surface of the pond, silvery ripples shimmered and spread, stirred by the hidden movement of life beneath. I found my place at the base of the willow, set down my pack, and pressed my spine gently against her massive trunk. My body ached from yesterday's exercise, but to my surprise, my legs folded into the cross-legged position with more ease than before.

There were no dark thoughts, no looming dread of another panic episode. The memory of the run—and the knowledge that I finally had a guide—brought a quiet sense of safety. Hope, it seemed, was a powerful remedy.

I let my hips relax and drew my posture upright against the tree. A long, slow inhale…letting the breath expand my belly, then rise into my chest. Shoulders soft. Neck loose. I lightly pressed the back of my head to the tree, feeling my spine lengthen. I continued the breathwork Guruji had taught me.

For a moment, I wondered what I was supposed to think about during this practice. No answer came—so I let go of the question and gave my mind permission to drift.

The birdsong wove itself through my thoughts, drawing me deeper into stillness. A warm, floral scent drifted on the air—spring blossoms mingling with the deep, mineral perfume of the pond. It was like the first rush of ocean air when you arrive at the shore. For a moment, I forgot I was in the city. It felt as though I'd stepped into another world entirely.

I breathed. Sat. Listened. Time folded in on itself.

After what must have been ten minutes, I slowly opened my eyes—and there, not six feet away, stood a tall, snow-white heron at the pond's edge. Perfectly still.

I froze, not willing to break the spell. Awe rose quietly inside me. The heron stood like a sculpture cast in marble. She tilted her head slightly, and one pale blue eye was fixed on me—watching. A moment passed, then, with stunning speed and precision, she struck the water with her long beak and emerged with a slender, silver fish, still wriggling.

The heron tilted her head back, and the fish disappeared down the length of her long neck. She stood for a moment longer, calm as a breeze—then she opened her broad wings and launched upward with a thunder of feathers. A gust of air fanned across my face. A jolt of exhilaration coursed through me—a thrill that made me want to leap to my feet in praise of the great bird. Her wings must have spanned four feet, lifting her effortlessly skyward with powerful strokes, until she vanished over the treetops.

The encounter left me in excited wonder. How majestic, how impossibly graceful—and all of it unfolding right here in the middle of so much human activity. Yet my thoughts, surprisingly, turned to the fish.

We don't often spare the unremarkable fish a second thought, and yet we marvel at the bird that consumes it. Life is the heron and the fish. For something to live, something else must die. Even in nature's most breathtaking displays, the cycle is unrelenting. I understood this was the way of the world—but that didn't make it any less sad. Is it possible to live in peace and harmony while knowing suffering exists all around us? In nature's beauty lies a fragile balance. Even the heron, ruler of the pond, isn't immune to fate—an eagle's talons or a passing car, should she land in the wrong place, could end her grace in an instant.

Everyone and everything has its days numbered. Even the sun, our great giver of life, will one day burn out. Not today. Not for billions of years. But the point remains: this day is all we have. That must be enough…if we like it or not, that's irrelevant.

The fragility of life made me think of the old woman in the hospital elevator. She was once young, vibrant, full of strength. Now her body was weary, her time nearly spent. What had she endured? What had softened her, broken her, and changed her?

Life holds all the majesty of the heron, but all the vulnerability of the fish. And perhaps, understanding that—accepting it—is another step toward peace.

I glanced at my watch. It was time to get on with my day. I climbed onto my bike and rode slowly out of the park. I just couldn't stop thinking about the heron…and the fish.

***

It had been a long day of running errands—I even found time to throw in a haircut. The image of myself in the elevator mirror had stuck with me, nudging something inside. I wanted to start caring again—not just about how I looked, but how I moved through the world. There was no doubt I'd let myself go over the past year.

Despite it being the most active day I'd had in a long time, I noticed something surprising: I didn't feel the urge to nap. That alone, felt like a small victory. Starting the day early, doing my breathing exercises in the park—it had all given me an energy that hadn't been there in months. New habits. That was key. And this time, they felt like a lifeline, not a chore.

I rolled up to the front of my bungalow and hopped off my bike. Running a hand through my freshly cut hair, I paused at the walkway and looked over the front of the house. I still remembered the thrill of seeing that SOLD sign staked into the lawn. It had taken years of overtime and relentless saving to finally put down roots in something of my own.

My dad had called it a "fixer-upper," and he wasn't wrong. But back then, I wasn't worried—a few summer jobs had given me just enough skill to consider myself handy. It turns out, I got busy…and not very handy.

Still, there was so much to love about the place. It sat on the corner of a quiet street, with no immediate neighbors—just a tiny sitting park on one side and an empty lot on the other, too small to develop, now overgrown with maples, cottonwoods, and tall, wild perennials that had made it their home. I'd once dreamed of homesteading here, of building a food forest and growing vegetables and fruit trees. But like so many dreams, that one had quietly slipped away.

Now the yard was tangled with stubborn shrubs and overgrown cedars in desperate need of trimming.

As I stepped onto the porch, I glanced down at the wooden stairs. They were weathered, peeling—they needed sanding, staining, and care. Just like everything else.

Maybe, I thought, it's time to start caring for the house too—not just myself. The truth was, I'd been letting everything slip.

I opened the door, still tempted to notice the neglected corners of my home. I'd fallen in love with this place for its simplicity—small, manageable, and uncluttered. My dad had always been a bit of a packrat, and I swore I'd never become like that. I needed space—not just physical, but mental. Owning too much weighed me down. That's why this little house was perfect. With fewer square feet, there was less room for the unnecessary, less space to hoard what no longer served a purpose.

"Wouldn't be costly to furnish, or time-consuming to maintain," I remembered saying to the previous owners when I'd toured it for the first time.

My favorite spot was the one I stood in now—what I fondly called the sitting space. It was nearly empty, save for an old brown leather couch and a polished wooden coffee table my parents had given to me when I moved in. The room caught the morning light perfectly, each sunrise painted the walls in gold. It was my quiet little observatory— the one place where I could sit and simply be.

Thankfully, I'd always been a tidy person, so the house was free of clutter. But even tidiness couldn't mask the wear. It was clean, yes—but tired. A bit like me, I thought.

I passed through the sunlit room and into my small kitchen, where I made myself a light snack. I didn't want to be too full for my evening run—something I was oddly excited for. The very idea of looking forward to a run felt like a good sign. After all, losing my breath—suffocating—had terrified me over the months, and now I welcomed the challenge.

Outside, the late afternoon air had cooled slightly. A gentle breeze moved through the rippling clouds, brushing the sky with delicate motion. I glanced down at my old sneakers and made a mental note: I need new runners. But between jobs, this wasn't the moment for new expenses. These shoes would have to carry me a little further.

I stepped down the stairs, stretched for a moment, and set off.

I aimed to run all the way to the willow tree and back—about thirty minutes each way—and maybe add the six-kilometre park loop that included a few hills. I liked the idea of building some strength in my legs and exploring more of the park's corners. There was still so much of it I hadn't seen.

I followed the same route I'd cycled earlier that morning, focusing on my breathing from the start. I pictured the Japanese man's slow, purposeful

59

stride—back tall, a slight lean forward, as if he were floating. I mirrored his posture and adjusted my breath. A smile tugged at my lips as I imagined his cheerful face again, running with joy written across it.

My legs felt surprisingly light despite the past two days—running, biking, seated posture work—it was more activity than I'd done in the last year combined. It felt incredible to move again. Guruji had emphasized that the body must function at our personal best, and already, I could feel my thinking sharpen. Why had I ever stopped? The reward was immediate. My father had warned me not to let myself slip, and now I understood the truth in his words: self-care wasn't something to squeeze in when convenient—it has to be the foundation everything else rests on.

As I trotted toward the park, I noticed something curious—everyone I passed smiled warmly at me. It wasn't until the fourth or fifth person that I realized I'd been smiling the entire time. Without knowing it, I'd been radiating joy. The Japanese man's influence lingered—I was moving slowly, breathing deeply, living in a way that invited connection. We really do shape the world around us.

At the red light by the bookstore, I caught a glimpse of the old woman inside, mid-conversation with a customer. I didn't want to interrupt. Just then, I noticed dozens of delicate blue butterflies resting on the flowers outside her window. As I stepped closer, they lifted into the air, scattering, and vanished into the breeze. I smiled and kept going.

The sun was low by the time I reached the park. My legs were heavy, so I skipped the loop and headed home. The sky transformed into a wash of gold and rose, the setting sun casting soft light across my cheeks. By the time I stepped through my door, the robins were singing their dusk songs, and a crescent moon was climbing on the horizon.

After a warm shower, I changed into loose sweats and a soft white T-shirt—perfect for my evening practice. I lit a stick of sandalwood and settled cross-legged against the wall, mimicking my posture at the willow. The incense drifted through the room, and I sank into deep breathing. The side effects of the medication seemed distant, nearly gone. Perhaps motion was medicine after all.

Twenty minutes later, I stretched my legs, and moved into the kitchen. A cup of tea, a light dinner, and I was ready for bed. It had been a long and meaningful day. I wanted to meet the next one early—beneath the willow, where everything felt a little more complete.

The Dream

Your vision will become clear only when you can look inside your own heart. Who looks outside, dreams—who looks inside, awakens.

—Carl Jung

The sun was setting, and the sky rippled with shades of violet, rose, and orange. Menacing storm clouds gathered overhead, slow and deliberate. I was walking a muddy trail along a steep mountainside in a light but persistent rain. I didn't recognize this place—I'd never been here before.

Though dusk still lingered in the sky, the forest was already thick with shadow. The trees and shrubs were only silhouettes, wavering in the dim. A subtle dread crept in. I felt pursued. I turned to look behind me, but the path dissolved into blackness—nothing clear, a thick void where I had come from.

The way ahead was no better: fading, obscure, and unsure beneath my feet. I kept going, breath ragged, the slope steepening. The trail gave way to sludge, and I dropped to all fours, scrambling, clawing for traction. The shrubs arched low with the weight of rain, slashing at my face and legs as I forced myself forward. My breathing quickened. The darkness behind me pressed in like a rising tide. Panic surged.

And then—I remembered.

My breath.

I drew in a long inhalation, filling my belly, then my chest. Again. And again. Slow and deep. With each breath, the path returned to view. My breathing steadied, and with it, the sense of pursuit melted away. The darkness was still there, but it had lost its threat. It was simply present.

Suddenly, the trail dropped away beneath me. I slid down a miry slope, and landed in a wide-open meadow. The rain had stopped. The air was clear. The massive willow stood at the heart of the field, its silver-green canopy shimmering in the twilight.

Here, the sky stretched open. The sun had just dipped below the horizon, setting the heavens ablaze in hues of fire and rose. Stars peeked through the indigo veil, and a crescent moon hung low, pale and new. It was like stepping into a hidden world—untouched, enchanted.

I moved through the tall grass toward the willow, and as I did, a flurry of tiny blue butterflies lifted into the air. Their wings caught the last rays of light, sparkling like embers of sapphire.

Beneath the tree was a still pond, and standing in its shallow water was a great white heron. Towering, motionless. Her eyes—piercing light blue—locked

Sean Lewis

onto mine. Her beak, the color of a dying sun, did not move, but I heard her speak.

Her voice was calm, serene, yet it reverberated through me:

"Only those who are prepared to look deep inside of themselves can find this place. The journey develops the eyes needed to see the destination. Without the path, the destination cannot be seen."

As the final word echoed within me, the meadow began to blur.

In an instant, I was back on the muddy trail. The rain fell in torrents. Darkness surrounded me, closing in from all sides. The willow was swallowed by shadow. I took a step forward, searching for ground— but my foot slid out from under me, and I fell hard onto my back.

I jolted awake.

I was in my bed, soaked in sweat. The sound of real rain drummed against my windowsill. I lay there, breathing heavily, heart still racing. Every detail of the dream remained—as vivid as waking life. I stared at the ceiling, trying to make sense of it.

Eventually, I drifted back to sleep.

Old Lost Stories

It is better to live your own destiny imperfectly than to live an imitation of somebody else's life with perfection.

Bhagavad Gita

I awoke just before sunrise, surprisingly well rested despite the intensity of the night's dream. Still in my pyjamas, I prepared a cup of tea and stepped outside to sip it in the cool, fragrant morning air. The sky was beginning to blush with soft pastels—pink, orange, and red—carrying with it the quiet mystery of what the day might hold.

The colors reminded me of the dream again. That strange, vivid journey felt less like fiction and more like a reflection of the waking life I'd been living these past months. This fear—the shadow that haunted me—always circling, always close, whispering of suffocation and oblivion.

Sitting under the willow had offered me something different. A stillness. A thread of peace. But in the dream, the very tree had become shrouded in darkness. Why? And then there were the heron's words—still echoing with uncanny clarity: *"Only those who are prepared to look deep inside of themselves can find this place. The journey develops the eyes needed to see the destination. Without the path, the destination cannot be seen."*

Too coherent for a typical dream. And more meaningful than anything I'd ever conjured from sleep before.

Maybe the meds were coming out of my system…maybe this could be one of the signs Guruji spoke of—could that be? He said that when your intention was clear, signs would appear. But did he mean only in waking life—or could dreams serve as guides too?

I drank my tea slowly and walked barefoot down the steps, the dew chilling my toes. The wet grass felt grounding, as if the earth were reminding me I belonged here. Birds filled the quiet with bright morning song, and when the sun finally crested the horizon, it spilled sudden gold across rooftops and treetops alike.

I breathed it in and made a quiet promise to myself: Let today be another day of discovery.

The dizziness was gone. The brain fog lingered, but lighter—like a veil that might soon lift.

Back inside, I changed into cargo pants and a sweatshirt, then packed my backpack with water, nuts, and chopped vegetables. I planned to stay out most of the day and wanted to be prepared. I took my usual route on the bike, the rhythm of the tires over pavement grounding me again in the present.

The old woman's shop was still closed. I made a mental note to return later to pick up an incense holder.

Something about today felt important. Like another thread in a tapestry, I couldn't see yet, but one that was slowly starting to take form.

This afternoon would also mark my first session with the psychologist—someone I'd booked over three weeks ago on the recommendation by my old friend Max. I missed him more than I expected. He had packed up and moved out west not long ago—the only friend I'd ever really opened up to—one of the few people who understood what it felt like to be buried under your own thoughts. Even when Max was struggling, he'd say things like, "you just gotta get out there and turn your own day around. No one's gonna do it for you." There was grit in him, but also compassion.

Before he left, we'd had one last long talk about life, purpose, and peace. He told me how working with this psychologist had led to breakthroughs he hadn't thought possible. "It's like I finally saw myself," he'd said, "and when that happened, I could see where I needed to go." After meeting Guruji yesterday, I'd begun to sense what Max meant.

I wondered if the dream's message tied into this—how looking deeply within could sharpen our vision for the path ahead. Maybe I'd bring that up in therapy today.

I felt grateful I'd managed to land an appointment. The doctor was well-regarded and wasn't taking on new patients, but in desperation, I'd written to him directly, explaining my circumstances. Thankfully, he agreed to see me.

I rode along the crushed stone path until I reached the heart of the park, where the willow stood motionless. The air completely still. Its long, trailing branches—like feathers—reached toward the pond, their reflections so perfectly mirrored on the water's surface that it was impossible to tell where the tree ended and illusion began. The boundary between real and reflected had dissolved. The willow, and its image were one.

The sun sat low in the sky, its early warmth softening the last of the morning's chill. I made my way around the pond and settled beneath the great tree. The grass was damp, but I didn't mind. Crossing my legs, I leaned back against the familiar trunk, and let my breath find its rhythm.

For about twenty minutes I practiced— breathing, straightening my back, loosening my shoulders. Though I felt calm and grounded, I still couldn't recapture the experience I'd had with Guruji.

As I sat quietly, a wave of nausea overtook me. It came on suddenly—violent, all-consuming. Certain I was about to vomit, I scrambled to the water's edge, heaving several times, but nothing came. The sickness was unlike anything I could remember. Again, I gagged, and again—nothing. Then came the dizziness. The trees, the pond, the sky—all of it spun. I felt too ill to panic. Curling into a ball in the grass, I lay on my side and tried to breathe. Deep, steady breaths. In through the belly, into the chest, shoulders down, neck relaxed. I clung to the rhythm, refusing to let my mind embellish the turbulence.

After about ten minutes, the spinning stopped. The nausea began to fade.

Damn these drugs. The side effects still lingered, and I had no idea how long they'd stay. It unnerved me. Was this going to be a recurring thing?

I reached into my backpack, pulled out my water bottle, and drank every drop—only then realizing how parched I was. My body slowly calmed. I could think again. Still shaky, I got on my bike and made my way toward the old woman's shop.

To my relief, she wasn't with any customers. She spotted me through the window as I leaned my bike against the wall, and her face lit up. I smiled back—genuinely happy to see her. There was a comfort in her presence, a quiet gravity that reminded me of Guruji. She radiated that same timeless peace. Around her, fear seemed to dissolve, and confidence took root.

Her long silver hair was tied in a braid down her back. She wore a sleeveless summer dress in earthy browns, greens, and soft beiges, patterned with frogs, butterflies, and birds that seemed alive in the fabric. She carried a heavy-looking box of books, yet showed no sign of strain as she set it down with ease.

"What brings you by so early on this beautiful spring morning?" she asked, brushing her hands gently over a tiny waist apron that she wore over her skirt.

"I just don't want to sleep in anymore," I said. "Mornings feel like the only time the world hasn't started pressing yet. I've actually been looking forward to them—I used to love mornings, and that seems to be coming back. Lately I've had this strange sense of purpose…even though I wouldn't say I've been very productive these days."

She nodded gently, waiting.

"I mean, I believe in work. Earning your way, making something of yourself—I've always believed that. I don't want to sit under trees for the rest of my life hoping the universe drops wisdom in my lap." I laughed awkwardly. "But lately…I don't know. I look around and see people charging ahead, building careers, achieving things—and a big part of me wants that too. This voice whispers that I'm falling behind, wasting time…that I'm missing out. Will any of it ever really satisfy me though?" I trailed off and swallowed hard. "Will any of it chase this darkness away that's destroying my life?" I actually teared up, hiding my face as I looked down at the floor.

She remained quiet, listening with her whole presence.

I fought past the emotions, "I don't want to reject the world," I continued. "I just want to find a way to be in it without losing myself. That's the part I can't figure out."

She began removing books from the box, her motions unhurried. The kind smile on her face never wavered. "Maybe it's not about choosing between purpose and productivity," she said softly. "Maybe it's about remembering that purpose can be found within what you're doing—even small, ordinary things—when you're present enough to feel it. Maybe you've been chasing meaning like it's a prize somewhere far ahead. But sometimes, the real work is learning to receive meaning in the moment."

She paused to stack a few books beside her, then added, "We're taught to measure our worth by results—salaries, achievements, progress reports. But your life isn't a spreadsheet, Rohan. You've been healing. You've been listening. That's work too. And maybe the reason it feels unfamiliar is because no one ever told you that this kind of work matters."

"I believe you," I said, looking down at my hands. "The last few days have been different. I've been waking early, going to the park, doing these breathing exercises Guruji taught me. Sitting under that willow tree, I feel…real. Like I'm finally hearing something inside me that's been buried for years. And it's not glamorous. It's not profitable. But it feels honest."

I glanced up at her, unsure. "But there's this voice—relentless—that keeps whispering I'm wasting time. That I'm falling behind. That everyone else is moving forward and I'm just… sitting still. And yet, when I am still, I feel something I don't feel anywhere else. A kind of quiet importance. Like I matter. But how do I know that's not just avoidance? How do I know I'm not just hiding from the hard things under the excuse of self-discovery?"

She held her gentle smile. "From what you're describing, it doesn't sound like you're avoiding responsibility at all. It sounds like you're being deeply mindful of this opportunity—the chance to change. Yesterday, you spoke of *noticing things*. What do you feel is different?"

I nodded slowly, my answer coming before I could fully shape it. "It's hard to explain. It's not one thing I can point to—it's more like a shift. A loosening. I feel connected instead of separate, like I'm part of something larger. There's a calm that comes with it. Not the kind of calm that means everything's perfect—more like the sense that I belong here. That life is speaking, and I'm finally listening."

I glanced at her, surprised at my own honesty. "It only lasts a few seconds, but when it happens, everything feels joined together—like the lines between me and the world disappear. When I met Guruji, I'd passed his building countless times before, but that day was different. Walking down the hallway toward his apartment, it was like I stepped into a moment that was waiting for me. Like I was meant to be there."

I paused and let the words settle. She didn't interrupt. Her silence gave me permission to keep going.

"And being here with you…" my voice softened, "feels like that too. Like I've known you longer than just two visits. When I'm around you, I feel…safe. Like I'm not alone. Like I'm part of something that stretches far beyond what I can see. I don't know why I never felt that before. I've passed your shop a hundred times."

She nodded thoughtfully. "That's very much our discussion from yesterday—sometimes it's not the world that changes, it's us. And when something inside shifts, our eyes begin to recognize what was always there."

She let the thought hang before asking, "Can you think of another time recently when something long familiar suddenly felt different?"

I smiled. "The park," I said without hesitation. "It's always called to me, but now that I've actually entered it…I feel the same thread running through it. When I saw the white heron yesterday, I felt so alive—so awake. That moment was so powerful, it followed me into my dreams."

The woman paused from sorting books and glanced over. "A white heron, you say? That's quite the message."

I looked at her, puzzled. "What do you mean?"

She walked to a shelf and drew out a thick, well-worn hardcover bound in soft brown leather. The gold embossing on its spine had faded with time, and a ribbon bookmark—its edges frayed— peeked from between the pages. She held it with an ease that spoke of long familiarity.

"For much of human history," she began, "people saw the natural world not as scenery, but as a living, breathing web of presence. Trees, birds, clouds—everything—was believed to carry spirit, wisdom, intention. In some cultures, that belief never went away."

She held up the book. "The idea isn't that animals or trees speak in words, but that the world communicates through sensation—through what stirs in us when we pay attention. You might not hear anything with your ears, but when you feel a strange stillness or a subtle pull, something is being said."

She placed the book on the counter. "You don't need to take it all literally. Just slow down enough to notice what the world stirs in you. Sometimes it takes a grand sunset or a mountain view, to feel connected. But other times, it could be as simple as a walk around the neighborhood. But one thing is certain, if your mind is always rushing ahead, you miss the little transmissions that the world is constantly sending you. But when you're still, something shifts. You begin to feel the thread that ties everything together."

She opened the book and flipped to a page. Turning it toward me, I saw a sketch of a white heron.

"This one," she said, tapping the drawing, "has long been a symbol of patience and inner watchfulness. In some traditions, the heron is thought to carry the wisdom of the Buddha. It reminds us to care for the still, sacred parts of life—and to listen when something within us awakens."

As she paused, I reflected on how foreign this kind of talk felt to me. No one in my world ever spoke of messages from the wild. I'd always loved nature, but I never thought of myself as connected to it—not in this way. My body and mind had always felt like a sealed unit—just another object among objects. But in the last two days that illusion had begun to crack.

She continued, "We've abandoned the old stories—the ones that once helped us understand our place in the world. These days, we turn to science and technology for answers. And yes, they serve many purposes, but they'll never show you your soul. That's a journey only you can take."

She paused, running her hand down the page. Nodding. Thinking.

She continued, "The stories passed down for thousands of years carry wisdom of those who walked this path before us. To discard them is to lose the map. If we let the lost rewrite the narrative of life, is it any wonder we feel lost ourselves?"

She took a deep soft breath, "You spoke of not feeling complete—this is what happens when society's pursuits neglect the deeper needs of the spirit. But these new habits you've begun— breathing, moving, noticing—these are not small things. They're ancient steps. They're part of the way back. You're standing between two worlds: the one you were trained to believe in, and the one that's beginning to nourish you. Don't be fooled by the noise about 'productivity.' You don't have to reject the world. You just need to find your rhythm in it. Your peace will come when your duties and your spirit begin to walk together. This will take patience and listening for those internal signs that resonate with the world you wish to create."

"Patience like the heron!" I blurted out, excitedly interrupting her.

"Precisely," she confirmed with a long slow nod of her head, "Now you're catching on about these signs," she said, with a big smile.

She placed the book back on the shelf and turned to me with a warm gaze. "You speak like someone who's begun to listen. That's rarer than you think."

I smiled. "I'm not sure what I'm listening to half the time. I just try to remind myself that listening helps me to change. And I can say for certain, something's definitely changing."

She extended her hand. "I'm Angelique."

I took her hand, feeling the warmth in her touch. "Rohan."

She held my hand a moment longer than expected, like she was taking in more than just my name. "It's good to meet you properly, Rohan. I sensed we'd speak more deeply, in time."

I nodded, now feeling even more comforted by her presence. "Thank you—for the talk, and for listening."

"You'll come to see," she said, returning to the books, "sometimes, we just need someone to remind us of what we already know."

Just as I turned to leave, I remembered. "Oh—do you happen to sell incense holders?"

"That one might suit your needs." She said, as she gestured to a small carved wooden tray near the counter. The end was shaped into the gentle curve of an elephant's head, the features softened into something almost human. I traced the intricate lines with my fingertips—Lord Ganesha.

I purchased it, slipped it into my backpack, and stepped back into the spring air. The sun was just beginning to warm the sidewalk. As I went to my bike, I looked through the window one last time. Angelique was still sorting her books, calm and focused—as if she hadn't just shifted something deep inside me.

I got on my bike and rode away slowly, the feeling of connection still lingering like the scent of sandalwood on my clothes.

Dr. Hernandez

". . .[the man who confronts his shadow] knows
that whatever is wrong in the world is in himself,
and if he only learns to deal with his own
shadow he has done something real for the
world."
— Carl Jung, Psychology and Religion

I rode my bike to the train station and locked it up before heading to the platform. Though it was rush hour, the station wasn't especially busy. I watched people disembark from the train across the tracks—polite, practiced, orderly. My train arrived shortly after, and though plenty of seats were free, I chose to stand, leaning against the door to practice my posture and breathing exercises. I pressed my back flat to the surface of the door, and drew my chin in, lengthening my spine, letting air fill my belly, then rise into my chest.

What I thought was discreet exercise, apparently wasn't. I noticed I had attracted the attention of a couple nearby who were whispering and glancing over at me. It probably looked odd, but there were no excuses, and I had to get the work done.

After a few minutes, I took in the faces around me. How many of these people were quietly fighting their own battles? On antidepressants? Caught in mental stress no one could see? We've all become experts at hiding what's going on inside—sometimes even from the very people who could help us. I'd done that for years. At least I'd finally taken steps. I just hoped today's appointment wouldn't be another letdown. Guruji had been different—like a fluke discovery more than a choice. I wasn't sure I'd get that lucky again.

At the next stop, more people boarded. I wondered how many of them felt they were pursuing their life's purpose. All this rushing, all this pressure—was there even a way to meet our obligations and still walk our true path?

Angelique's words came back to me: "Your peace will come when your duties and your spirit begin to walk together." I didn't want to abandon my responsibilities, or live small just to feel calm. I wanted a life I could be proud of—one that stretched me, challenged me—but not at the expense of the quiet place inside where peace lives. Maybe that's the real work: not choosing between purpose and peace, but learning how to carry both without one crushing the other. Not checking out of life, but learning to walk through it with calm intention.

The train arrived at my stop early. I stepped out into the sunshine and walked the four blocks to the office slowly, letting the spring warmth settle me. But even without an obvious trigger I felt that all too familiar mental static begin—ruminations.

What if he wants me back on meds? I'd have to admit I quit cold turkey. The nausea. The brain fog. That the panic attacks still creep in. He'll think I'm unstable. He'll want to talk to my doctor. I can see it now, he's going to call Guruji a cult leader, or say Angelique's just a mystical fluff?

My heart rate spiked. I was spiraling. My breathing grew shallow, and the suffocating feeling returned. I sped up, trying to shake it off—and stepped into the street.

Tires screeched. A horn blared. Someone shouted obscenities.

Only then did I realize I'd crossed on a red. I ran to the other side and collapsed against a lamppost beside a trash bin, dizzy, shame-heavy, expecting to vomit.

That's when the image of the great willow rose in my mind—its branches dipping gently into the still water, the leaves catching the morning light, shimmering silver-green in the wind. The air was sweet with the scent of flowers, and the chorus of birdsong wove through it all. The scene wrapped around me like a steadying hand, loosening the knot in my chest. For a moment, the noise inside me quieted.

81

Never before had I been able to summon an image of peace so quickly—it was a portal back to stillness.

I held onto the willow in my mind, and began the breathwork—deep inhale, belly expanding, air rising into my chest. Again. And again. Slowly the panic loosened its grip. My feet felt the ground. My mind returned.

I have Guruji. I have Angelique. This psychologist won't take that from me. Maybe—just maybe—he'll even help.

With each breath, I brought myself back to now. To what is. To what's good.

By the time I reached the address, I'd calmed enough to walk in. The office was in the lower level of a converted duplex, its front step worn smooth by years of visitors. As I reached for the handle, a small plaque caught my eye: DR. CALVIN HERNANDEZ. Beneath it, a second note, simple and unexpected: Please remove your shoes and have a seat in the waiting area.

Inside, the space was peaceful and unexpectedly inviting. Four chairs sat in a cozy, well-decorated room. Plants were scattered throughout, and light from a large stained-glass window poured in, casting soft prisms across the sanded wood floor. The window depicted a knight on horseback plunging a lance into a snake-like-dragon—vivid, old, symbolic.

A tall bookshelf stood in one corner, lined with volumes on psychology, alongside some light novels and magazines. Soft classical music hummed from a hidden speaker beneath a thick fern. A misting globe on a black side table released a steady stream of lavender-scented vapor. The heavy wooden door to the back office was lined with thick rubber trim, for deliberate silence.

I closed my eyes and sat up tall, drawing a slow breath and letting the lavender seep deeper into my chest. Inhale the healing air, exhale the fear. The music seemed to lengthen each breath, coaxing my thoughts into stillness. My gaze wandered—to the globe, the ferns, the knight. "Lost stories," I murmured aloud, the words curling into a quiet smile.

The sound of the door opening pulled me from my reverie. A man stepped out—around sixty, medium height, with olive skin, and a buzz of silvery grey hair. Lean and composed, he wore a close-cut white short sleeve, and slim black pants. Despite his sharp appearance, he radiated calm, unforced warmth.

"I'm Dr. Hernandez—but please call me Calvin," he said, extending his hand.

"Rohan. Nice to meet you," I replied, apologizing for the dampness of my palm. The aftereffects of the panic attack still lingered faintly.

"No worries," he said with an easy smile. "It's warm out. The windows are open—you'll cool off in no time."

He ushered me inside, and I settled into a black leather armchair facing him. Behind him, a large bay window framed an ancient oak, just beyond the glass, its branches filtering the sunlight into a soft, golden wash across the room. Dr. Hernandez sat opposite me in a swivel chair—relaxed, yet fully attentive.

The office mirrored the waiting room—bright, earthy, and deliberately composed. Abstract paintings in black, red, and yellow punctuated the white walls. Along the far side, ceremonial masks made of wood and clay stared out, their carved expressions shifting from joy to sorrow to rage. One with wide eyes and drawn lips, seemed almost afraid. Plants filled the corners and shelves, their silent presence lending the air a steady calm. Between us, a low glass coffee table held only a single box of tissues—an unspoken invitation.

"Thank you for agreeing to see me," I said. "I know you're busy and not really taking new patients. My friend Max—who you worked with—had great things to say about you. He thought you might be able to help."

"Yes, Max was a wonderful man," Dr. Hernandez replied, his tone warm but measured. "I'm glad he connected us. I'm looking forward to seeing what we can discover together. Your message gave me a good starting point—why don't you tell me a little more about yourself?"

I gave him a brief overview of my background—how I'd grown up in the city with loving parents, no siblings, and what I considered a fairly normal home life, aside from the occasional rough patch. Despite frequent bouts of depression, I managed to finish school with average grades. I never found much passion in academics, but I did have a knack for problem-solving—a skill that eventually landed me a role in quality control management.

"I've always been good at understanding problems," I told him. "Just… not so great at figuring out what I actually want to do with my life."

I mentioned my love for reading, gardening, and how much I used to enjoy exercise—before things unraveled—but that I was finding my way back to it all. Then I admitted, almost as an afterthought, that three days ago I'd thrown away my antidepressants and decided I was done with them.

For a moment, Dr. Hernandez didn't speak. His eyes held mine, steady but unreadable, as if weighing how much of that choice came from conviction—and how much from exhaustion. Then he leaned forward.

"You say depression has been a recurring thing in your life. What does that look like for you, Rohan?"

"Ever since I was a kid, I've gone through these phases where I couldn't focus. This vague sense of dread would settle in—like something awful was about to happen, though I could never say what. It just lingered, a dark cloud hanging in the background. Sometimes it stayed for weeks. I noticed it especially when I was enjoying something. It's like the more joy I felt, the more this shadow would move in and pull me away from it. Suddenly I couldn't focus on anything but the fear or the sadness, even if nothing was actually going wrong."

I hesitated, then continued. "It's strange how my own thoughts could feel as real as actual events—like they carried their own gravity. And as I've gotten older, it's been more frequent. It's always there, just enough to remind me it hasn't left. The thing is, I love life. I'm actually a pretty optimistic person. I don't take it out on people or walk around in a bad mood. I try to be kind, even when I'm hurting. Sometimes, if I make an effort to smile or engage with people, it even lifts me a bit. The sadness doesn't feel like it comes from the outside. It feels like...like some character inside me. Unpredictable. Uninvited."

Dr. Hernandez leaned back, thoughtful. "It sounds like you carry two truths at once—that deep optimism and kindness, but also this shadow-self that intrudes."

I paused. "I feel like I just get in my own head too much. The chatter doesn't stop. I start imagining negative scenarios—things that might happen—and then I can't let them go. I feed the thought until it grows so heavy, it feels real. My body reacts like it's already happening."

Dr. Hernandez nodded and asked, "Do you feel that by predicting problems ahead of time, you can somehow prevent the turmoil they might bring? And are your predictions often accurate?"

I gave a half-shrug. "I guess I worry so often that I'm bound to get it right once in a while. But that's luck not foresight. At work, problem-solving feels natural—almost easy. But outside of work, in my own head, it's like I invent problems out of thin air. I get caught rehearsing disasters that haven't even happened—and most likely never will. I waste all this energy fixing something that only exists in imagination."

He smiled gently. "We call that rumination. Repetitive thinking isn't always harmful, but when the loop feeds anxiety instead of clarity, it starts to drain you. It steals your focus, your peace of mind. You end up trying to fix problems that don't even exist, which is exhausting. In fact, rumination is one of the most common fuel sources for depression."

I nodded slowly, already feeling seen.

87

"You mentioned that your thoughts feel like real things," he continued. "Some people live closer to their thoughts than others—and I'd say you're one of them. That's not a flaw. It just means we need to build strategies that help you step back, so you can see thoughts for what they are: mental activity, not prophecy. He paused, letting the words sink in. I often remind clients: thoughts are not things. We'll return to that idea often."

Dr. Hernandez paused a moment, then asked, "It sounds like anxiety has been with you a long time. Tell me more about the panic attacks. Do you know what triggers them?"

"It depends," I replied. "Sometimes they come when I'm quiet and thinking—like they sneak up on me out of nowhere. Other times, it's when I'm overwhelmed, especially when something feels out of my control. That's when the surge hits. It sounds strange, but I think I live with two kinds of panic: one that creeps in from silence, and one that slams down when life feels too big to hold."

"That doesn't sound strange at all," he said, leaning forward with interest. "In fact, you're not the first person to describe it that way."

"Really?" I blinked. "Others feel that way too?"

"Most certainly. People from all walks of life—young, old, successful, struggling—speak of panic and anxiety in different 'flavors.' It's rarely just about what's happening around us. More often, it's about what remains unsettled inside. That's where the real discoveries lie."

He let the pause breathe before adding, "Tell me more about the way your two kinds of attacks feel different."

I waited a moment to gather my thoughts. "When I'm overwhelmed with worry about future scenarios, my breathing grows shallow, my chest tight. It feels like I'll forget how to breathe—like I'm actually going to die. I know it's irrational, but I can't turn off the voice that keeps predicting disaster. That kind of panic, at least, I can name. It's stress. It's fear of what might happen."

I took a breath and looked down at the floor.

"But there's another kind," I said quietly, swallowing hard as my mouth became dry. "It's harder to explain—and far more terrifying." I glanced at the mask, fear etched across its face, "It doesn't come from fear about the future. It comes when I'm still. When I sit quietly, when I'm about to fall asleep…when the noise of life finally quiets. That's when I feel like I'm slipping into a dark void, like I could vanish inside my own mind and never come back. The calm turns hollow—empty. As if silence itself is trying to open a door I'm not ready to walk through. It feels…like death is rising up in me. Not dying in the physical sense, but dissolving into something I can't control. And I don't want to look at it."

Dr Hernandez nodded—his eyes steady on mine. "That does sound frightening," he said softly. "But notice this: no matter how dark the feeling, you've always found your way back. That tells me you already have more resilience than you realize."

The words caught me off guard. They didn't feel like flattery—they felt true. And for a moment, the heaviness in my chest eased.

"I often feel ashamed of how I'm turning out in life," I admitted quietly. "It's good to hear there might be something I'm not failing at."

My gaze drifted past him to the oak tree beyond the window, its branches steady in the light. I couldn't hold his eyes—too much of me felt exposed. My chest tightened at the admission—the same prickling exposure I'd felt waiting for Dr. Chan, seeing the man in the hospital gown. Exposed in his own way. Naked in mine.

The room was quiet. A silence long enough for years of held-back thoughts to stretch out and finally settle—no longer rattling inside me, but resting somewhere useful instead of destructive. That's when I told him about Guruji—how the breathing exercises had steadied me—though I left out the stranger parts of what I'd experienced.

He let the quiet linger—giving my words space to breathe—he tilted his head, voice low and steady. "Why do you feel ashamed, Rohan?"

I shook my head. "I don't even know. I've had steady jobs, I finished school—even if I wasn't exceptional. But sometimes I catch myself picking apart the lives of people who seem to be thriving, almost wishing to find cracks beneath their success. It's petty. It's not something I'm proud of. I think it comes from being so tired of always feeling like I'm the one who needs fixing. I just feel so weak."

Dr. Hernandez leaned back slightly, his expression soft. "You're not being petty, Rohan—it's human. When we're hurting inside, sometimes the only relief is to imagine that others, too, are carrying secret burdens. It doesn't make you cruel—it just means you're weary of carrying your own weight without recognition."

He offered a small, steady smile. "You say you feel weak? No, Rohan. Bottling up your emotions, pretending nothing's wrong—that's not strength, it's denial. Real strength is exactly what you're doing right now: facing yourself. Taking responsibility for your inner life. Most run from that. You're not. You're watching your own mind, noticing patterns others spend a lifetime ignoring. That's not weakness—it's awareness. And awareness," he leaned in slightly, "is the only way real transformation ever happens."

He eased back in his chair, not rushing to fill the silence. The pause stretched, steady and unbroken, until his words arrived softly. "This shadow you've described…have you ever felt it wasn't only tormenting you, but trying to tell you something?"

I looked up, surprised by the question.

"What if I told you," He continued, "that you're not broken at all—but that you're brushing up against a rare threshold. This void you fear may not be the enemy, but an invitation. You just haven't yet been prepared to meet what it holds."

"I really don't know what to say Calvin," I admitted. "To think of this darkness as special feels like a huge leap. My doctor wanted me on antidepressants just to stop the torment. The psychiatrist even wanted to double the dose—turn me into a zombie."

He rocked back in his chair, folding his hands loosely. "If you're willing, I'd like us to try a different approach. What if, instead of fighting the darkness we turn toward it? Looked it in the eye. I promise you, Rohan—you won't be swallowed by it. On the contrary. You'll find yourself seeing more clearly, moving more freely. And from that clarity, a truer path may finally emerge."

"Truer path," I repeated, almost under my breath. The words felt familiar, stirring an echo. "Guruji said something like that too—that when your intentions are clear, signs begin to appear, confirming that you're on the right path."

Dr. Hernandez smiled. "And doesn't that feel true? The moment we grow clear inside, the outer world bends to meet us. Strangers arrive who were never strangers at all. Paths appear where once there was only fog. Think of your last few days—Guruji, me—we emerged as if summoned."

He gestured toward the oak outside. "Change your inner lens, and the world becomes a new landscape. The hero doesn't sit idle, begging for the way to be lit—he steps out, and the path reveals itself under his feet. That's how we discover the life that was waiting for us all along."

My mind shifted instantly to the message of the heron in my dream. This sounded undeniably similar—I kept it to myself.

I sat quietly with that.

"I still worry about becoming some kind of dreamer, chasing only what feels good. I want peace—but I don't want to abandon my responsibilities either." I said, having difficulty making eye contact.

"And you shouldn't," Dr. Hernandez said. "This isn't about rejection of duty. It's about integration. The life you envision—the one that brings peace and meaning—can only come with effort, work, and accountability. The key is noticing:

are my choices moving me closer to that vision, or farther away? Even the missteps help shape the person you're becoming. The journey is in the trying."

I nodded. "That makes sense." Then hesitated. "I've been meaning to ask. Do you believe dreams have meaning? I've read that some psychologists take them seriously."

He folded his hands over his chest. "Some do, some don't. I do—especially the dreams that linger, that carry emotional residue into waking life. They're uncharted territory, yes, but they often carry truths that haven't found words yet."

I exhaled, relieved. "Good. Because I've been having recurring dreams—vivid, intense—and the same darkness that haunts me when I'm awake is in them too."

He nodded thoughtfully. "Let's get into those next time. Dreams are maps too, if you know how to read them."

He checked his watch. "Let's meet again in two days. The early sessions are where the groundwork happens, and it's important that you feel supported while the terrain is still unfamiliar."

I agreed completely. "Is there anything I should do before then?"

"Keep doing what you've already started. Write down your dreams in as much detail as you can. Continue your mindfulness practices—but without judgment. Catch the thoughts you'd like to change, acknowledge them, and let them pass. Don't punish yourself for having them. And move your body. After all the anxiety, meds, and restlessness, you'll need physical movement to restore balance."

"I've been jogging again," I said. "And my posture and breathing exercises—they've helped more than I thought they would."

He stood and shook my hand, placing his other hand firmly on my shoulder. "Keep going. Trust in the work and in yourself. You're not just trying to get better—you're learning how to live fully. I'll see you in two days."

As I stepped back onto the sidewalk, the street felt unfamiliar. I hadn't realized how disoriented the panic had made me. Now, the world looked different. And across the street—there it was. A bohemian import shop I hadn't noticed when I arrived. Hanging in the window was a vivid tapestry: a half-man, half-elephant figure, wreathed in flame.

"Lord Ganesha," I whispered. I stared at it, not knowing what it meant—only that it meant something.

Sean Lewis

The Shadow

Anger can be a wonderful wake up call to help you understand what you need and what you value.

— Marshall B. Rosenberg

The train ride home gave me time to reflect on my session with Dr. Hernandez. It had gone far better than I expected—far better than I feared. In fact, I felt hopeful. Like maybe, just maybe, I'd found someone else who could really help me.

I couldn't help but notice that once again, my worry had been dead wrong. He hadn't scolded me for quitting the antidepressants cold turkey. He hadn't questioned every strange thing I said. He just listened. And calmly guided me through it. The more I thought about it, the more I realized: when my worrying mind gets ahead of me, it only ever stirs up turbulence. But when I take mindful action—like Guruji taught—something shifts. Each small step reveals what comes next.

I reached my stop and headed down to retrieve my bike.

Gone.

Vanished.

The bike stand was empty—except for the lonely fragment of my busted lock dangling like a broken wishbone.

I stared for a moment in disbelief before it hit me like a punch to the gut. "Blast you, damn bike thief!" I blurted out, loud enough to earn a few gasps from people nearby.

One woman yanked her child by the arm, clutching his ears, giving me a sharp stare. I offered an apologetic wave, half-smiling. She did not smile back.

I started walking toward the bus stop, a cloud of fury gathering overhead. My inner monologue turned dark fast. I imagined the thief— a greasy, smug bastard—riding away on my beloved bike, like some petty king of the city. I hoped he hit a pothole and flew over the handlebars. No— maybe a car! That would teach him.

"What kind of sick person steals someone's bike?" I muttered out loud again. A pair of elderly women shot me disapproving looks, like I'd stolen *their* bikes. I quickened my pace, mildly ashamed but still seething.

The bus pulled up just in time to save me from more public outbursts. I climbed aboard, paid my fare, and dropped into the only open seat, still mentally plotting the thief's downfall.

I was deep in my fantasy of karmic justice when I finally looked up—and there she was. An elderly woman standing right beside me, clinging to the overhead bar like a windswept pine tree. I had no idea how long she'd been standing there. I jumped to my feet. "Please—take my seat," I stammered. She smiled and thanked me warmly.

And just like that, the guilt hit. How long had I been stewing in my own anger, totally blind to what mattered most to me? Honouring the elderly had always been something I valued. But there I was—too wrapped up in imaginary revenge to notice a real human being right in front of me.

That was the moment it clicked. This—this was a sign. When you're out of alignment with your values, the world doesn't need to send a thunderbolt. It just sends a bus ride. A missed opportunity. A simple reminder that your thoughts are steering you off course.

I remembered what Dr. Hernandez had said—don't punish yourself for your thoughts, just notice them. Acknowledge. Gently course-correct.

I took a deep breath. In through the nose, belly expanding. Out through the mouth, releasing all that sickly tension. No more cursing bike thieves. No more imaginary car accidents.

The path is the practice. Even when it means walking home without a bike.

The Subconscious

By the time I arrived home, the sky looked like it was gathering breath for a storm. Mentally drained, I decided to skip my run and do my posture and breathing instead. After a hot shower, I lit a sandalwood stick and placed it in the new holder I'd picked up earlier. Dressed in sweats and a loose white T-shirt, I took my usual spot against the wall, sitting cross-legged—more easily now—straightening my back, inhaling deeply into my belly, then into my chest.

The scent lifted my mind and softened the weight of the day. A calm spread through me—steady, simple. Guruji had said transformation begins in the body, and I was starting to believe it. Just these small rituals—walking, pedaling, filling my lungs with breath—had cleared more fog than months of thought ever had.

After ten minutes of breathwork, I stood with ease and drank two tall glasses of cool water. I'd read somewhere that hydration flushed toxins, even traces of medication, from the body. I wasn't sure how true it was. Still, drinking it felt like a simple ritual of cleansing—something I could control.

I opened the bedroom window and climbed into bed. The rain began. Thunder rolled softly in the distance. A cool breeze drifted in carrying the scent of lilacs and wet grass. I lay quietly, letting the hush of the storm lull me to sleep.

And then—the dream returned.

I was back in the stairwell. I recognized it.

There were no windows here. Just cement walls pressing in from every side. The halogen tubes overhead flickered faintly. The metal stairs clanked underfoot, each step echoing like I was in the hollow of a giant cavern. The air was still and thick, as though it hadn't moved in years.

I knew this place. I'd been here before. Many times.

There was something I was supposed to do— someone I needed to meet, somewhere I urgently needed to be—yet with every step I descended, I was moving further away. It's like the staircase was swallowing me whole. The air felt thinner the deeper I went, squeezing my ribs tighter with each landing.

A low hum seemed to vibrate through the concrete, like a hidden engine. I reached a narrow landing. Five steps below, a single door waited. It had no markings. No handle. But I knew it led me somewhere I wouldn't return from.

An invisible pull urged me closer. Like a gravity of the soul.

Time was ticking. I needed to leave. Now.

Suddenly, I was no longer on the stairs. I was on a bus, moving away—farther and farther from the place I was meant to be. I didn't remember getting on. I didn't remember choosing the direction. The other passengers—faceless shadows, still as mannequins waiting in the dark—the driver unseen. Outside the windows: crooked buildings perched on a dark slope, dim streetlamps glowing like distant fires in a fog. Bare trees scattered like forgotten skeletons. The loneliness felt like cement on my chest. I knew this road. I had ridden it many times. Always away. Always too far.

The dread built in my body. A knowing: if I didn't get off this bus soon, I would never get back. Time was ticking. Still, I sat paralyzed.

The road narrowed. The streetlamps vanished. Blackness wrapped around the vehicle, an impenetrable gloom. I was standing alone in a concrete pit—no exit, no oxygen—a heavy iron plate dropped overhead like the lid of a tomb.

I screamed—but no sound escaped.

I woke up with a gasp, chest tight and damp with sweat. The cool air from the open window felt soothing, and slowly brought me back. Outside, the sky was brushed with soft purples and streaks of peach.

Just a dream. But the pressure lingered.

The door. The staircase. The return that never comes. Time ticking.

Something still waiting. I don't know how long it took, but I finally fell back to sleep.

***

The storm had passed, and morning sunlight spilled into the room. I sat up in bed and let the unease from the dream roll off me like fog lifting. My second session with Guruji was in three hours, and with no bike to ride, I decided to walk to the Bliss Centre. The long walk would do me good.

I drank two tall glasses of water and made a cup of tea. Stepping onto the front porch, I breathed in the clean scent of the damp earth. The memory of the dream still clung to me—its strange weight and urgency often lingered for hours, sometimes the entire day. Max used to call them dream hangovers. He wasn't wrong.

I wanted to be in a good headspace before meeting Guruji, so I left early with the intention of sitting beneath the willow tree for a while before the session. I packed some snacks and water, and placed an envelope of money in my bag—enough for two sessions. It felt right to give him the same fee I'd paid Dr. Hernandez.

I dressed simply: sweatpants, T-shirt, sneakers. Who knew what physical challenge lay ahead.

On my way through the neighborhood, I passed Angelique in front of her shop, chatting with a man and woman. When I caught her eye, she waved with a warm smile. What a wise woman she was. I'd walked past her store countless times without a second thought. It had always been there—but I had not. Something in me had to awaken before I could see what was right in front of me.

It struck me again how perspective reshapes the world. As Guruji had said—and Dr. Hernandez echoed—once we become clear on what we're seeking, life begins to conspire with us. People, places, and moments appear as if summoned by intention. Angelique, the shop, even this morning's walk—they weren't accidents. They were threads of a pattern still revealing itself.

Still, I wondered: how could I ever know if I was making the right choice? How can I tell the difference between a helpful sign and a tempting distraction?

Then **Dr.** Hernandez's voice echoed in my head: What it must do is bring you closer to what you envision as a life of meaning.

That was it. If the path aligned with what I truly valued, then I had to trust it—even if it didn't feel immediately easy or comforting. Some of the best choices, I was learning, don't soothe right away. They ask for patience, for faith in the ache, until meaning begins to take shape.

By the time I reached the park, a strong warm wind had picked up, sending white petals from the spring blossoms sailing through the air like soft, slow snowflakes. The city's morning stir faded behind me as I wandered deeper into the green, the grass wetting my shoes with dew.

I settled beneath the willow, back pressed against its trunk, legs crossed. Facing the pond, I closed my eyes and began to breathe—slow, full, deliberate. My shoulders dropped. My belly rose and fell. Across the water, the wind carried petals like tiny dancers, landing on the pond with barely a ripple.

The tension from last night's dream began to lift. I imagined what it might be like to be the willow—rooted, unmoving, a quiet witness to seasons and life. No striving, no rushing. Just stillness.

No urgency…no urgency…

105

My mind cleared. I felt a subtle energy expand outward, but then—just as suddenly—the familiar darkness surged. It rose like a tide, eclipsing my calm. Black smoke coiled into tentacles reaching from the depths of my mind, attempted to absorb all thought. My eyes shot open. Sweat broke across my skin; I shivered. But this time, I didn't run. I stayed. I breathed. The petals continued to fall. The world went on. And so did I.

Slowly, the trembling faded. Fear loosened its grip. I slipped back into stillness—once again, the silent observer. Time drifted.

Then, on the far side of the pond, the Japanese man appeared again, trotting in his grey cotton sweatsuit, same bright white shoes flashing. Even from a distance, his grin was unmistakable. He caught my eye, beamed wider, and raised a finger, pointing to his temple, and raised a thumb high. I laughed and returned the gesture. My mind felt good. Almost light.

For the first time, I had stayed with the shadow without falling into panic. I watched the man disappear over the hill, and smiled to myself. Maybe I was finally learning to walk the path.

The Light

The walk took me about an hour, but there I was, standing at the corner and looking across the street at the same sign I'd seen just four days ago. Then, I'd come hollowed out and clinging to hope. Today, I felt something entirely different—anticipation. In less than a week so much of my inner world had shifted that even the city around me seemed changed.

I crossed the street and entered the building. That familiar voice answered the intercom and buzzed me in. The elevator was as slow as I remembered, dimly lit, but now it brought a strange sense of peace. I closed my eyes and breathed deeply, filled with quiet gratitude—for Guruji, for Angelique, for Dr. Hernandez.

Just days ago, I had been drowning in isolation. But now…now I could see a way forward, not alone, but with guides beside me. Guides. That word felt right, as if it belonged to me.

Warmth moved through my body, and time itself seemed to pause. I breathed in freedom—not

107

a grand, abstract freedom, but something intimate. A loosening of knots. A lightness. A freedom from the thick fog of an unwell mind.

The elevator jolted to a halt. I opened my eyes—and froze.

The mirror showed not my face, but a colossal figure: half-man, half-elephant, its trunk swaying lightly, its gaze torch-bright. A pulse of fear shot through me. Then the doors opened, spilling light across the glass, and the apparition dissolved as if it had never been.

I stood there, shaken. Last time an aged man. Now…I didn't want to say it. Best not to name a trick of the mind. I rubbed my temples, whispering, "These meds…still clawing their way out."

The familiar scent of sandalwood greeted me again as I walked the hallway to the Bliss Centre door.

Guruji opened it before I could knock. With palms pressed together, he bowed. I returned the gesture smiling.

"It is very good to see you, Rohan," he said warmly, closing the door behind me.

I removed my shoes. "I've been looking forward to this since our last session," I said.

He studied me with a glint in his eye. A quiet knowing. "You look more peaceful. Your breathing is calmer." He gave my shoulder a gentle pat of recognition.

"I've been practicing my posture and breathwork every day," I said with pride. "Sitting cross-legged is getting easier, but…" I hesitated. "Whenever I begin to relax, the darkness comes back. That presence. The one that stirs the panic. It still comes."

Guruji nodded, unshaken. "Come," he said softly. "Sit. We will talk about that in a moment."

I sat down on one of the red cushions, facing Guruji and the carved wooden statue of Lord Ganesha. My legs folded easily now. The battle scene in the tapestry beneath us felt familiar, like a place I'd passed through in some other lifetime.

I glanced at the statue. The vision from the elevator still lingered—half-man, half-elephant, watching me from the glass. Should I tell him? I didn't want to seem like I was reaching, chasing mystical experiences. For now, I would keep it to myself.

I took a deep breath and scanned the room, grateful for its grounding stillness. The same quiet peace wrapped around me, just like the first time I'd been here. My eyes landed on the tapestry of the two white herons. Angelique had said Buddhists believed they carried the wisdom of the Buddha. I realized then—I didn't actually know what that meant.

"Guruji," I said, eyes still on the herons, "what is the wisdom of the Buddha?"

He followed my gaze and nodded with a small smile. "Many speak of the Buddha," he said. "Some wisely, most loudly. There are scholars who debate, and spiritual performers who dress the part. But the Buddha himself—he was a man of doing, not talking."

He shifted slightly, settling into his cushion.

"Simply put, he saw that our attachment to the world—especially to our limited sense of self— is the root of suffering. But he also taught that life, though impermanent and dreamlike, is to be lived. Fully. He didn't teach escape, but balance. A joyful responsibility."

"Is that what's meant by the middle path? I've heard that mentioned before?" I asked.

Guruji's hands formed a gentle shape in the air as he spoke.

"There are always two extremes: indulgence and denial. Certainty and confusion. Hope and despair… The middle path is about pausing between these—it doesn't rush to cling or to reject. It listens. It waits. It chooses with clarity, not impulse. We hold loosely, not from apathy, but from clarity."

He smiled, leaning in slightly. "You must understand: the middle path is not a theory—it's a way of walking. To dress like a sage, to quote the holy texts, to hang beads on your neck—these do not make you awake. The moment you believe they do, you are further asleep."

I chuckled quietly.

"Buddha was human," he said plainly. "He struggled, tried many ways, made mistakes. But he never stopped walking. That is what made him wise. He didn't try to make others follow his path—he showed that we each must walk our own."

His voice softened.

"Talk is easy, Rohan. Talk can become a trap. But action…action is truth in motion. When you act from a place of stillness, you will begin to know peace—not the word, but the experience."

There was a pause. A shift in the room, like something unseen had just entered. I shivered.

"Now," he said gently, "let us breathe together, and return to our place of tranquility."

Guruji closed his eyes and took in a long, deep breath—like the first time we met—his entire torso expanded. The inhalation lasted what must have been ten seconds. Without opening his eyes, he whispered, "The key to a long breath is patience. Inhale slowly through the nose—not in one big gulp. Draw the air in gently, as though pulling it from the depth of your sinuses. Try to reach fullness after five seconds, letting it fill your belly first, then your chest, as you have learned."

I followed his instructions, and after a couple of tries, I was surprised at how much calmer I felt. The simple shift—slowing the inhale—had an unexpectedly powerful effect.

As I sat breathing slowly, I noticed something new—my body was holding itself. The spine, once desperate for support, now stood on its own. Ease had replaced strain. A quiet proof that something within me had begun to change.

Guruji opened his eyes. His face looked serene, like someone waking from a restful nap.

"Why does the darkness frighten you, Rohan?" he asked.

The question caught me off guard.

"Because I'm afraid of getting trapped there," I said. "Imagined or not, it feels very real."

He nodded slowly, his eyes warm with understanding. I could see that he knew exactly what I meant. It was the second time in two days I had described that inner place of terror—and again, I wasn't met with confusion or clinical detachment. No one was suggesting I was broken. Maybe I wasn't crazy after all. Maybe I wasn't alone.

I took the moment to tell him about Dr. Hernandez—how he wanted to guide me into the void, to confront it directly.

"That just sounds like a horror show," I added with a nervous laugh.

Guruji took another breath and gestured gently. "Let's return to the breath. Close your eyes. Inhale for five counts. Hold for five. Exhale for five. We'll do it together."

We breathed together, and a wave of stillness moved through me, warm and quieting. My thoughts dissolved, leaving only awareness. Then I noticed a shift. My sense of self no longer rested behind my eyes—it had floated forward, as though my very consciousness now hovered at my brow. In that space, a light flickered into being, delicate as a firefly, dancing at the bridge between my eyes. Its glow felt calming, strangely known, like a memory just out of reach.

I wondered briefly if it was just light from the room leaking through my eyelids—but the moment I had that thought, the light vanished.

When I opened my eyes, Guruji opened his too, as if he had been waiting for the exact moment.

"You became distracted," he said, without any hint of judgment. His smile was soft. "Tell me what you experienced."

"It was calming," I said. "My mind felt…empty. Not in a blank way—more like peaceful. Still. And this sounds strange, but…it felt like I wasn't inside my head anymore. Like I was just a tiny point floating outside my forehead."

I hesitated. It sounded ridiculous now that I said it aloud. But Guruji listened without blinking, his smile unchanged. There wasn't a trace of doubt in his expression—only attention, and something that felt like quiet recognition.

I continued, "Is it possible that I saw a tiny white light…right here?" I touched my forehead, still feeling a bit self-conscious.

Guruji nodded. "It's quite possible. Some would say you glimpsed the opening of your spiritual awareness. Those who like labels might call it the 'opening of the third eye' or the 'crown chakra.' But names only limit the experience. Once we define something, the mind starts to believe it understands—and then stops seeking."

He touched his own brow lightly. "This energy centre—between your eyes—is tied to inner vision, spiritual well-being, and the wisdom that guides you beyond thought. When it's blocked, anxiety rises. We feel lost, disconnected. The mind grows restless."

"How does it get blocked?" I asked.

"Depression. Deep sadness. The sense that your life has no clear purpose. These are heavy veils over the spirit. But it's clear you're beginning to lift them. If only for a moment, you saw the light—and that's no small thing."

He leaned forward slightly. "Let me ask you, Rohan—just now, when you saw the light, were you in the darkness?"

I paused, surprised by the realization. "Yes. But…I wasn't afraid."

"And why not?"

"Because I wasn't thinking," I said. "I was just…breathing."

Guruji smiled. "Exactly. Thought brings fear. When you're fully present, even the darkness is safe. Thought ties you to the material world. It clings. It anticipates. But in that moment, when the mind went quiet, your awareness was free. That's the beginning of real peace."

He sat back and folded his hands. "These ideas will grow clearer in time. For now, know this—your healing has begun. And your work with Dr. Hernandez will help too. You've lived with a racing mind for so long, and he too will guide you in slowing it down. Yes, we are spiritual beings—but we live through the body, and carry the scars of

115

our psychology. Therefore, we must train the mind gently, like tending a wild horse—not with force, but with presence."

I nodded, taking it in.

"We don't aim to control the mind," he added. "Control leads to suppression. Instead, we observe it. A calm mind doesn't need to be dominated—it stays centered because it's being witnessed. And no, the goal isn't to become emotionless. Emotions are human. Beautiful, even. But they must be harmonized with the life we seek."

He looked at me warmly.

"We won't always succeed. That's not the point. Progress—not perfection. Perfection is a myth in the physical world. True perfection only exists in the nonmaterial world. Spirit doesn't demand perfection—only that we keep walking the path."

"Guruji, what do you mean by 'perfection only exists in the non-material world'?"

He took a deep breath and closed his eyes. "Close your eyes once again, Rohan. Breathe deeply and allow your mind to become clear. Gently push away your thoughts and feel the warm emptiness around you. No thoughts. No direction. No up, no down. Just weightless…and floating."

I followed his voice and slipped inward. No thoughts. No self. Just the sensation of floating in a place beyond all form. Somewhere in that stillness, a hum began to resonate—soft at first, then stronger. It wasn't a sound I could trace to the room. It was everywhere and within. A vibration that pulsed through my entire body, gently shaking me free from pain and worry.

The edges of my skin dissolved. There was no "me". No distance, no in-between. Just a perfect whole—one hum, one field, one essence. It was familiar, though not from memory. It was more like something I'd forgotten I always was.

Time no longer moved in moments, but in waves. Each breath rose and fell as if the universe were breathing me. Colors flickered behind closed eyes—gold, indigo, a soft white glow that throbbed in rhythm with the hum. My heart felt as though it had opened wide, not to let something in, but to reveal that nothing had ever been outside.

For a while, I simply floated there, neither waiting nor wanting. A sweetness hovered at the edge of the silence, tender and complete.

The clear chime of a bell shimmered through the air—dull and muffled—as if beneath water. I knew it was calling me back, though I felt no urgency to leave. There was no journey back, just a shift. Heaviness returned. My skin tingled as sensation re-entered. The air felt thick. I opened my eyes.

Guruji sat where he had been, now holding a small gold bell.

"Welcome back, Rohan. You did not become lost—you knew where your body was all along. You cannot lose yourself once you know that you are everywhere."

I glanced at my watch. Nearly twenty minutes had passed. "I'm sorry…I think I fell asleep? It felt like I was dreaming, but…not dreaming."

"You lost awareness of time, which means you entered timelessness. You were not asleep. You were fully present, just not attached. You touched what we call *Atman*—your eternal self. That is the perfection of your non-material form: consciousness without identity, being without thought."

His words rang through me with unsettling clarity.

"We will explore this more," he continued, "as you walk toward your highest potential. Remember, the path to peace begins with the pursuit of excellence—body, mind, and spirit. This week, we began with the body and the spirit. In time, Dr. Hernandez will help you tend the mind—

just as other guides may offer their gifts along your journey. No single path holds all the answers."

I felt myself returning, piece by piece. "Guruji," I said, still half in awe, "was that the same place I felt the first time I met you? That strange presence—was that *it*?"

He smiled but said nothing, only nodded as if I had answered my own question.

A faint hum lingered in the room, not so much as a sound but a presence. When I looked directly at Guruji, it deepened—not louder, but steadier, I wondered if he had carried me there, not only through breath, but through some current that moved beneath thought. Was there an ancient practice that allowed him to touch the edges of my awareness? I didn't ask. To speak might have broken the spell.

Whatever the source, I knew now that the boundaries I had once believed in—of mind, body, and fear—were not unbreakable. They were bendable. Malleable. And I could begin again.

I exhaled slowly and met Guruji's gaze. "What else can I add to my exercises this week?" I asked, my voice carrying a new kind of anticipation.

Guruji gave a wide smile. "Yes, Rohan. In just four days, your posture, breathing, and flexibility have improved greatly. You've been an attentive student. Now it's time to build strength."

Guruji gestured to the mat beside him. "Come, Rohan. Let me show you the baithak. This is not merely a squat— it is an ancient calisthenic. It will ground your body and strengthen all of your most important muscles."

He stood and motioned for me to follow. "Keep your spine tall," he said. "Start with the feet flat on the floor. Feel the equal distribution of your body weight on each foot. Bend the knees and lower yourself to the floor keeping your feet flat. When you rise, return to standing, but now on your toes—the balls of your feet. It is much like the squat—that you are no doubt familiar with—but performed with grace and breath. The arms are not rigid. They flow with the body. Fingers touching the floor as you descend, then reaching for the heavens as you stand. Fluid as a palm leaf gently fluttering on a breeze."

He demonstrated: feet shoulder-width apart, arms outstretched, squatting deeply as the fingertips swept toward the ground, then rising with a fluid motion—lifting the arms and the heels in a single upward wave.

"Now we do twenty together."

We began the sequence, and to my surprise, the movement felt more natural than any squats I'd done before—less mechanical, more alive. Each repetition was like a breath for the body. But by the final few, my thighs and calves were on fire. Guruji, of course, looked as composed as ever.

"Now we go to the floor," he said gently moving. These are what we call, *dand*. Similar to the push-up but more dynamic." We entered a downward dog-like position, hips high, then swooped forward—chest low, ending in a cobra pose—before returning to the start.

"Ten repetitions. Breathe deeply through the nose, into the belly." He said without any strain in his voice.

These were much harder. My arms trembled with the final few repetitions, and I was relieved when we finished. Guruji looked like he could have done ten more.

He walked to a narrow bureau in the hallway and returned with a small sheet of paper. On it were illustrations of the two exercises.

"Keep this," he said. "Every morning, twenty *baithak* and ten *dand*, followed by your seated posture and breathing. Always inhale slowly—five seconds in, five seconds hold, five seconds out—all through the nose."

I folded the paper carefully and tucked it into my pack. "This is so exciting, Guruji," I said, rubbing my triceps.

He gave a knowing smile. "We've only just begun. There's still so much more to share. I'll see you in four days."

I reached into my bag and removed the envelope with my payment, placing it at the base of the wooden statue of Lord Ganesha.

"Guruji…may I ask, who is Lord Ganesha? I've seen his image a few times lately."

He closed his eyes and breathed in deeply. "Lord Ganesha is the most beloved deity in our tradition. He is the remover of obstacles and the patron of new beginnings. Whenever we set out on a journey—especially one of transformation—we invoke his presence. Not to remove hardship entirely, but to give us the strength to face it. You are walking the same streets, Rohan…but everything feels different. That is the nature of inner change. Resistance will arise in places it never did before. You'll need new tools, new awareness. Lord Ganesha reminds us that every path worth walking begins with difficulty—but no difficulty is without its teaching. When you face obstacles, bring his image to mind. Let his strength become yours."

We bowed to one another, palms pressed gently together. I turned and stepped back into the hallway. It was silent and still, as if the air itself had paused to listen.

All Things Must Pass

When I stepped out of the apartment building, a current of energy ran through me—the same quiet, electric optimism I had felt the last time I left Guruji's company. The world looked brighter somehow. My body felt light and unburdened, as if a layer of static had finally gone silent.

I walked quickly, heading for the park. The brisk pace did wonders—just like running, it cleared the fuzziness I still carried from the meditation. That otherworldly dream-state had left its imprint on me. Though I tried to cling to the experience, it was already fading—like a dream remembered vividly on waking, then dissolving moment by moment. One part stayed with me though: a certainty, deep and clear. My mind and body had caused me to forget what I really was.

Before I knew it, I had arrived. The familiar bend in the path, the scent of spring blossoms. I crested the hill, expecting the gentle welcome of the willow—and stopped short.

There was a crowd.

A dozen, maybe more—people of all ages gathered near the tree. Some were visibly upset, voices raised, others murmuring among themselves. A tall older man in green overalls stood calmly in the middle of the group. I could see it now: a bright orange mesh fence encircled the willow like a warning ribbon. My heart sank.

A chill ran through me. The sensation was instant and uncanny—my dream of the shadow overtaking the tree came rushing back. The feeling that something had happened. Or was about to happen.

I moved closer, trying to make out the conversation.

"Why are you cutting it down?" A woman asked, her tone sharp.

"I'll be writing the city councillor, the moment I get to the office," said a man in a suit, arms crossed.

"I'll be preparing a petition," an elderly lady added sternly, her voice trembling.

Cut the tree down? I felt my chest tighten. This can't be happening. She's the most beautiful tree I'd ever seen.

The man in overalls lifted a hand, speaking gently. "I've cared for the trees in this park for thirty-six years, and this willow was likely here a hundred years before me. She's as dear to me as she is to all of you. Please believe me when I say—

we've done everything we could. We brought in a specialist. We considered bracing the limbs. But…she's dying. Her branches are splitting. It's only a matter of time before one falls. If it hits someone…"

He paused. "She's lived her life. I know it hurts. But it's time."

A hush fell over the crowd. My eyes welled with tears. I didn't care who saw. I stepped to the edge of the mesh barrier and placed a hand on the orange plastic. Then, just as Guruji had taught me, I drew a deep breath into my belly and let it expand into stillness.

I looked up into the canopy, her leaves rustled softly in the breeze. Some branches, I now noticed, were bare. The bark on her great limbs was peeling, exposing weathered wood beneath. Two massive branches near the trunk showed clear cracks, like quiet wounds too deep to mend.

It was true. And somehow that made it worse. I turned and glanced at the crowd. Their voices softened. The outrage had faded into quiet understanding. Some stood with arms folded, others in reverence, stealing glances toward the tree—as if saying goodbye.

I started my walk back home, no longer feeling the desire to practice my exercises. All I could feel was a sense of loss. In a strange way, I felt like the old tree was part of what was saving me. Sitting beneath her branches by the pond had helped me feel grounded, like I was finally beginning to find peace in a way I so desperately needed.

After wandering aimlessly for what felt like hours, I found myself across the street from Angelique's shop. She was outside sweeping the front walk in a long white summer dress, patterned with butterflies and birds, a turquoise head scarf tied at the back. When she saw me, she paused and waved, her expression softening with concern.

As I crossed the street, she asked, "Why do you look so sad, Rohan?"

"The great willow in the park is sick. The city has to cut her down." I tried to hide it, but the sadness cracked in my voice. "Why does it seem like every time things start to get better, something comes along to remind you that the struggle isn't over."

Angelique sighed gently. "That truly is sad. I understand how you feel. But struggles are part of the healing. Sometimes they space themselves out, giving us time to breathe. Other times they come one after the other with no pause between. That's just life. Not a punishment, not an omen. Just life being life. And how we face those struggles defines the kind of life we live."

"I guess I'm just scared. That willow was where I felt safe. When anxiety hit, I'd go there. Now it's going to be gone. I know it sounds selfish."

"That peace you found beneath the willow isn't lost," she said. "That peace is inside you, Rohan. The tree simply reflected it back to you."

I nodded slowly.

"Even willows that live over a hundred years must eventually return to the earth," she continued. "We mustn't attach ourselves to what is impermanent."

"That's one of the wisdoms of The Buddha," I said, eyes lighting up as I recalled my conversation with Guruji.

She smiled. "That's right. Peace begins when we stop expecting permanence from things that were never meant to last. Everything physical returns to the source."

Kind of like the fish and the heron, I thought...life's fragility.

"What do you mean by the source?" I asked.

"The source is the great potential of the universe. It's the energy from which all things come and to which all things return. Nothing ends, Rohan. It transforms."

"Guruji said perfection only exists there—in that place beyond body and mind."

Angelique nodded. "The source is where all things are One. You are part of that cosmic journey. And while no one can walk your path for you, the more you walk in harmony with life's rhythms, the more you'll come to understand your place in the whole."

I hesitated, then asked, "If everything's impermanent, why love anything at all? Why open your heart just to eventually suffer?"

Angelique smiled softly, her eyes misty but warm. "Because love isn't about holding on—it's about being present. To love, knowing it *will* end…that's real courage. And that courage brings depth. Meaning. It shapes the soul. Yes, love can break us open, but it also fills us with a beauty nothing else can. When we avoid love to avoid loss, we lose twice—first the joy, then the growth. Attachment, plain and simple, is a fear of losing. Attachment is fear. But love…true love…knows how to let go, because it's not about possession. It's about becoming."

"I think I'm starting to understand," I said. "But it's not easy."

She placed both hands over mine. "It's not meant to be. Real growth takes years—through heartbreak, challenge, and the wisdom born of both. Rushing it only builds walls around your feelings. Let go too fast, and it's not letting go—it's avoidance. Take your time, Rohan. You're learning. And remember your dream: if you don't grow the eyes to see, you'll never recognize the destination when you reach it."

I took a deep breath. "Thank you. I finally have three people in my life who understand these things. I'm really grateful for that."

Angelique gave my hand a squeeze. "You'll find your place of peace, Rohan. Because peace isn't something out there—it's a connection to what's already inside you."

I hugged her and thanked her again and made my way home—feeling like something stronger had begun to grow inside me.

The Storm

You won't even be sure, whether the storm is really over. But one thing is certain. When you come out of the storm, you won't be the same person who walked in.

—Haruki Murakami

It was midday by the time I arrived home, and the sky was beginning to cloud over. Rain was in the forecast, but it was supposed to clear by early evening, so I was still hoping to get my run in.

I made a simple lunch of beans and soft tortillas. After eating, I brewed a cup of hot tea and moved to the sitting area, lighting a stick of sandalwood.

Guruji and Angelique's words were still drifting through my mind—detachment, third-eye awakening, impermanence. These notions had no foothold in the world that raised me. They weren't taught in schools, spoken at dinner conversations, or written in the plans I made for myself. They didn't belong in the curriculum of the life I once thought unshakable. And yet, some part of me was making room for them now, as if a door had always been waiting.

I sat with my back against the wall, legs crossed, and began a deep five-second inhalation through my nose. I held it for five seconds, then slowly released the air from my belly and chest. I repeated the rhythm again and again.

I closed my eyes and tried to recall Guruji's words: Thought brings fear. When you're fully present, even the darkness is safe.

Then I tried to remember the sound of his hum—the vibration that had seemed to dissolve the very edges of my being. That experience felt like a dream now, some impossible place far beyond what I could create on my own. Yet I knew what I had felt. I had touched a silence that held no thoughts…and no pain.

I took another deep breath, and when my mind grew quiet, something flickered—tiny at first, like a star pulsing far away. Then, almost instantly, it gathered at my brow, just above the bridge of my nose. I stayed with it, breathing. Thought dissolved. Warmth moved through my body, and for a moment it felt as though the floor itself had fallen away, though I hadn't moved at all. Only stillness. Only presence. A shimmer in the dark that felt both foreign and strangely familiar.

Without warning, a deafening crash split the air. My eyes snapped open.

Lightning flashed across the window, followed by a roar of thunder that seemed to shake the walls. The room had grown strangely dim—storm clouds pressing in, though it was only early afternoon. I glanced at my watch: 2:30 p.m. That couldn't be right. The tea beside me was cold. The incense had burned itself out. Somehow, more than an hour had passed, though it felt no longer than ten minutes.

Had I drifted into sleep? Was it only a dream? Or had I entered that same elusive space I'd entered with Guruji—the light, the warmth, the stillness that had no measure of time?

I didn't have the answers, but I knew one thing—I was alive with energy, humming from the inside out. The storm outside no longer felt threatening; it felt like an invitation. Rain or not, I needed to move.

I changed into my shorts, T-shirt, and sneakers, then stepped outside into the storm.

Rain was falling lightly but in a steady sheet. The sky was dark, streets hushed, with only the occasional car passing by. Puddles gathered at the sides of the road. Though it was only midafternoon, the air carried the dimness of early evening.

Wind swept through the trees, shaking water loose from the leaves so it fell in sudden bursts. Thunder rolled far off, and streaks of lightning split the swollen sky. Clouds churned above me—black, twisting, restless. It looked like a sky that warned of tornados, and yet, I began to run. Not fast—just steady, letting the oddly warm spring air and the rain soak me through.

My shoes slapped through puddles, splashing water high against my legs. The storm didn't resist me; it carried me. Each drop felt like a washing. Each stride, a loosening. It was a liberation. It was cleansing.

Angelique's shop appeared on the corner. Her wooden display tables that usually spilled out onto the sidewalk were gone, pulled inside, and the door shut tight. The windows were misted with condensation, trickles of rain weaving paths down the glass. I couldn't see in.

I pressed on, laughing aloud as thunder cracked and the lightning continued to tear ragged seams across the sky. The storm was now fully unleashed, the rain lashing at my face. I turned the corner, water splashing high with every stride, and sprinted across the street. A surge of energy carried me forward—into the waiting darkness of the park.

The gravel path had turned soft beneath my feet, leaving prints behind me as I covered ground. Wind tore through the trees, snapping small branches and flinging hundreds of helicopter seeds into the air. They spun and swirled in wild, unpredictable currents, caught in the storm's frenzy.

Each gust of wind stole a piece of me, scattering it among the branches, the rain, the spiraling seeds. I felt myself surrender, not resisting the turbulence, but letting it carry me.

I reached the center of the park and wiped the rain from my eyes. Where the willow once stood—towering, strong, a fixture of peace—now remained only a tangle of broken limbs and a massive split trunk. Half of her had fallen into the pond, great branches splintered and torn. Two of the largest limbs had crushed the protective fence, leaving it bent and twisted. The sight stopped me cold. It was a reminder that even what seems eternal can fall.

Thunder cracked again. Another flash of lightning—I gleaned something white near the fallen branches. I squinted through the storm. There, beside one of the larger fallen limbs, was the heron. I froze. For a moment, I feared she was dead—unmoving, her stillness unnatural.

Then her head turned toward me, and the crystal blue of her eyes caught the storm's light. With the next flash of lightning, her wings spread wide. She launched into the air, cutting through the wind and rising effortlessly into the sky until she disappeared into the grey mist of the storm.

As if by divine command, the rain ceased in an instant. A single ray of sunlight broke through the clouds, striking the pond and turning its surface to liquid gold. Slivers of light pierced through the canopy of trees, illuminating the broken willow in soft beams. For a moment, ruin and radiance shared the same stage.

I walked through the mud and sat in the wet grass with my back against the shattered trunk. I closed my eyes and drew in a deep breath, listening to the soft rumble of thunder retreating into the distance.

"Thank you," I said aloud, and sat with my thoughts. There are moments in life when we come across just the very things we need, and if we're paying attention, we can actually see them. This grand tree had been one of those things. A teacher—can I even say a friend?

I stood and placed both palms on what remained of the trunk. It didn't feel like enough—not for what she had given me—but it was all I had to offer in return. Just a touch—a letting go.

I turned to leave, water sloshing in my shoes, my clothes weighted with rain. My body soaked. My soul heavier. But something inside me had been lit. Somewhere in the wreckage of something I once leaned on, a spark stirred. Some of the things we lose are the very things that set us free.

***

I arrived home around dinnertime, took a hot shower, then changed into my cotton sweats and soft white T-shirt. I lit a stick of incense and played some quiet ambient music while preparing a light dinner of leftover beans, tortillas, and a simple salad.

I ate, seated on the floor, legs crossed, my back against the wall. When I finished, I stood up and stretched my arms toward the ceiling, surprised by the ease with which I rose from the floor. My back felt strong. My legs, warm and fluid. Something was shifting in me—quietly, steadily.

Tomorrow was my second appointment with Dr. Hernandez. A subtle unease clung to his suggestion to "go into the darkness and meet it head on." My time with Guruji had helped me glimpse the void more clearly, but I still didn't know what it truly was—or what Dr. Hernandez intended for me to face.

Even in moments of deep peace during meditation, it was as if something always lingered at the edges. A shadow in the margins, waiting to be brought into the light of consciousness. Guruji had said I must train my thoughts and understand my mind if I wanted to find peace. If I was truly committed to developing my fullest potential—

body, mind, and spirit— I had to go in open. If not without fear, then at least with courage.

I brewed a cup of tea and stood at the kitchen window. The storm had cleared. A half-moon glowed in a clean sheet of navy sky.

"What is my place in the cosmic journey?" Angelique's voice rang in my mind, clear as the night air. I had never asked myself that question before. Had most people? If I stopped and asked someone on the street, would they know? Would they even understand the question? I'd spent so much of my life doing what I was told mattered— school, work, security, approval. The metrics of a well-ordered life. But never once had anyone said, "find your place in the cosmos."

Now, I saw how vital it was. Each of us walks a different path—no two the same. We can have guides, mentors, companions along the way, but the road beneath our feet is ours alone. We see through our own eyes. We carry our own wounds and questions. And yet, as I sipped my tea, I wondered: do all paths eventually bend to the same place—back to the source Angelique spoke of, back to that perfect stillness Guruji described? The place no mind and body can enter, but the spirit never forgets.

When I sat with Guruji and felt that vibrant hum move through me, I'd brushed against something I couldn't explain. A presence, a memory, a clarity too pure to belong to the physical world. Maybe that was the place. The source. The perfection beyond thought. Yet doubt lingered. How could someone like me be having these experiences? Not long ago, I needed medication just to make it through the day. And now here I was, speaking of awakenings and altered states of consciousness. It felt surreal. Like I was watching my life unfold from behind a veil. Like I'd slipped into a dream I hadn't meant to enter.

Still, it was happening. And tomorrow, I'd continue the journey. Whatever the void was, whatever I feared—I would face it. With courage.

It was still early, but the day had been long, and something in me knew, rest was part of the work. I finished my tea, turned off the lights, and prepared for bed.

***

I awoke just before sunrise—5:35 a.m. exactly. I slipped on my sweats and made my way to the kitchen for two tall glasses of water. Then I opened the back door and stepped outside into the cool, inviting air. A soft blush of pink brushed the edges of the clouds that punctuated the morning sky. The birds were already in full chorus. I had never noticed how much louder and more varied their songs were in the spring.

Stepping onto the damp grass, I felt that inviting coolness rise through my feet—pleasant, grounding. I stretched my arms out wide, then overhead, and began my *baithak* squats. Up and down, my arms swinging in rhythm, creating momentum with each movement. After twenty repetitions, I dropped down into the push-up position and began the *dands*. I lowered my face toward the damp, soft grass, then arched upward, eyes lifted to the awakening sky, breath deep and steady.

On the first repetition, just as I looked skyward, I observed the silhouette of a great bird—its long neck tucked back against its body, long legs trailing, wings moving slow and deliberate. The soft light of the rising sun framed its body—shimmering white against the dark canvas of the storm-cleared sky. The heron. It glided gracefully above the rooftops, surveying the land as it passed. I smiled as it disappeared into the distance.

When I was done, I returned indoors, lit a stick of sandalwood, and drank two more glasses of water. I sat cross-legged against the wall and began my five-second breathing rhythm. Inhale...hold...exhale. My heartbeat from the workout gradually softened. Within minutes, I was fully at ease.

Sunlight spilled into the room in golden shafts. I opened my eyes just enough to see the amber rays landing directly in front of me. The incense smoke rose and drifted through the light, curling and dancing with effortless grace—no urgency, no resistance. Its form, invisible in the shadows but fully revealed in the sun. I watched it, enchanted.

I remained there for twenty minutes—just breathing, observing, existing.

It was still early, and my appointment with Dr. Hernandez wasn't until noon. I decided to pass by the park to see what the groundskeeper had done with the fallen willow.

I packed a water bottle and a few snacks, planning to walk as much of the day's journey as possible. As I placed the items in my backpack, I found the folded paper with Guruji's exercise diagrams. I smiled, thinking how I could have easily missed the Bliss Centre that day—that simple sign in the window. Meeting Guruji had felt like a defining moment in my life. It was hard to believe it had been so random.

Maybe, I thought, this is what Angelique calls a meaningful coincidence.

As I set the diagram on the small table by my incense holder, I noticed the paper had a printed letterhead. In the top right corner, it read:

**Guruji Mandeep—Bliss Centre 4444
Emerson Street—City Centre**

My eyebrows lifted. Did Guruji have another location? Emerson Street was familiar—within walking distance from Dr. Hernandez's office. I decided I'd pass by after my appointment.

Closing my eyes for a moment, I drew in one final deep breath. It was time to meet the shadow again. But this time, I knew…it would be different.

Big Andy from Donegal

Big old trees take root in our souls as much as they do the ground. People hold on to memories and experiences differently when they're around trees. They're magical things.

—Big Andy

I stepped out into the fresh spring morning. The sun was warm, and the calm stillness of the early hour could still be felt. A brisk walk to the park would do me good. Just enough movement to wake up the body, but not enough to leave me drained for my session with Dr. Hernandez. I passed Angelique's shop, but she was nowhere in sight.

As I neared the park, the trees came into view—tall silhouettes rising above the buildings, a sea of green stretching out before me. I felt a quiet excitement in my chest. Despite the occasional flare of anxiety, I hadn't felt this peaceful in …well, I couldn't remember when. The fog from the medication seemed to have lifted completely.

I reached the park sooner than expected, realizing my slow jog wasn't much faster than a brisk walk. The gravel crunched beneath my feet as I looked up, admiring the sway of the canopies overhead. Birds of all kinds darted through the air, busy with whatever affairs spring mornings demand. The scent of lilacs and magnolias lingered—a fleeting bloom that never lasted more than a few weeks, yet whose fragrance stayed with you long after it was gone.

When I reached the pond, I saw the willow was gone. The fallen branches had been cleared, the ground swept. I had expected to find a work crew still tidying up, but the space was already clean— almost as though the willow had never been. One massive branch, though, had been left behind, placed carefully on the bank, like a wooden bench. It stretched a good ten feet and was thicker than the trunk of any other great tree I'd seen. The underside had been cut flat so it could rest stably on the ground. I ran a hand along its bark. It was a sad sight, but I was grateful something of the willow still remained.

I sat on the branch, looking out over the pond. A few ducks paddled lazily, dipping their heads beneath the surface, then popping back up to shake water from their feathers. I smiled. A warm breeze carried pink crab-apple petals through the air, forming tiny islands on the surface of the pond, drifting aimlessly.

From the slightly higher perch, I noticed something I hadn't before—beneath the water's surface, a few giant carp glided, slow and unbothered. Then, to my right, I spotted four sticks protruding from the muddy shoreline, encased in a subtle mesh of chicken wire.

"I saw you here the other day in the crowd," came a voice from behind me.

I turned quickly. It was the kind groundskeeper—from yesterday.

He stepped beside me. "Willows root fast if you give'em enough water," he said, nodding toward the sticks. "We held onto those four branches yesterday when we took the rest of her down. Planted them just before sunrise. They'll take root soon enough, but we always plant four, just to make sure one thrives. Might even get a few more from the original root system if we're lucky."

I stood up. "Hard to believe those twigs could ever become as majestic as that old tree, right?"

He removed his cap and walked toward the young cuttings. "Aye, that's the thing with trees. You give them time and space, and they'll surprise you."

He turned. The man was built like a barn—wide shoulders, muscular arms, a thick neck. His silvery-grey hair was cut short over the ears, with long strands falling over his deep hazel eyes. He looked to be in his late sixties.

"I come from a long line of caretakers," he said. "My great-great-granddad came from the old country and started farming this land. My dad followed in the same tradition. I guess you could say I never stood a chance. In all seriousness, these trees, they change the way you look at the world. If you're not good in yourself—get out and be around trees. They'll heal you."

"I've been coming here every day for the last week," I told him, glancing to where the willow stood. "It's helped me a lot. I didn't know trees could actually make you healthier."

"They can," he said. "Trees breathe out what we need and take in what we don't. They clean the air, soften noise, and let out powerful healing products. Doctors won't tell you that, but if you get real quiet and get out of their way, a tree'll do its magic on ya."

"I thought my uncle was making that stuff up when he used to say that. I guess he was onto something. My name's Rohan."

He shook my hand with a grip like bark. "Another Irish lad? Well, you can call me Big Andy. Not for the reasons ya think. Hell, my name ain't

145

even Andy. All my friends gave me that name years ago. A Big Andy is what we call herons back in Donegal. Our legends say they watch over nature, and so do I. Been watching over parks here for more than forty years. I take the name as a compliment."

"I saw a heron here the other day," I said, feeling goosebumps on my arms. Part of me wanted to tell him about the dream and how the heron kept appearing, but I held back, not wanting to look strange. My dad used to say, *don't scare people off until they at least get to know you*. I chuckled, thinking of my father and his funny expressions.

I stayed quiet about the dream and the recurrence of herons lately, but I couldn't ignore the sense that this just wasn't another coincidence.

"Yea, they've been making a bit of a comeback these last couple of years," Big Andy replied. "We've got a small number up this way now. Where there's shallow water, tall grass, and a touch of quiet, you'll find herons—until fall, then they bugger off south for the winter."

I smiled. Big Andy was the kind of guy who made you feel like you'd known him longer than you had. He was easy to talk to—and even easier to listen to.

"We kept that big old branch from the willow so folks could still sit in her company like they used to," he continued, gesturing to the thick trunk I was resting on. "I know it's not the same, but it's the best we could do. You saw for yourself how the crowd responded to the thought of cutting her down. Big old trees take root in our souls just as much as they do in the ground. People remember things differently when they're around trees. They're magical, y'know. Offer me all the money in the world to do something else and I'd turn it down flat. Working around these beauties—well, it's as close to God as I get most days."

I nodded, feeling the truth in his words.

"Anyhow, Rohan, I'd best push off. We've got a delivery comin' on the south side—forty saplings are going in the ground over the next couple of days. So much more joy in planting than in cutting."

He paused, a gentle smile spreading across his face. "Reminds me of something I heard a long while back—can't recall from who: 'trees teach us to love and accept something just the way it is.' That one always stuck with me. We don't expect a tree to up and change—so why do we expect so much out of each other?"

With that, he tipped his cap, turned, and ambled away, his heavy boots crunching in the gravel as he disappeared down the path.

A Journey Inward

*Where we had thought to travel outwards, we
shall come to the centre of our own existence.*
—Joseph Campbell

It was ten to twelve when I arrived at Dr.
Hernandez's office. Glancing back across the street,
I saw the tapestry of Lord Ganesha still hanging in
the window. The remover of obstacles, I thought to
myself. I took a deep breath. The air seemed thicker
than usual, like the moment before a storm or the
hush before a confession. Some part of me knew—
today was different.

I stepped inside and settled into the waiting
area. The same tranquil music played, though this
time the globe released a cool mist tinted with mint.
The air itself invited me to relax—much like at
Guruji's center. I found myself imagining how I
might bring some of that peace into my own sitting
area at home. My thoughts drifted, until the heavy
door swung opened at exactly noon, breaking the
stillness.

Dr. Hernandez stood in the doorway with a broad smile. He wore a close-fitting black T-shirt and slim-fit black pants. His silvery grey hair looked freshly buzzed, same as before. "Rohan, good to see you. Please come in."

I took my seat opposite him, the same place as last time, facing both Dr. Hernandez and the large window with its steady view of the oak tree. It felt grounding. Anchoring. Sunlight filtered through the leaves, sending thin rays across the wall where the masks hung. The minty fragrance from the waiting area lingered here too, carrying with it the same calming air into the room.

Dr. Hernandez sat in his swivel chair and leaned back into the springy back support. "How have the last couple of days been, Rohan?"

I paused before speaking, as I had no clue where to start, or how to fill him in on recent events. "It's hard for me to say. Everything in my life now just feels so strange. New. I'm worried you'll think I'm even crazier than you already do."

Dr. Hernandez leaned forward, smiling. "I don't think you're crazy, nor will I ever think that, Rohan. Take your time and remember, no judgment."

"I just feel strange talking about these feelings and the problems that I have. I so often hear people around me say that we've all gotten too soft and need to toughen up. There's so much conflict and division in the world. My problems somehow seem…trivial, yet they cause me so much mental struggle."

I hesitated. Part of me didn't want to say it. Not out loud. But it came anyway. "I hate feeling weak and needy."

Dr. Hernandez nodded, rubbing his chin. "I understand what you're saying, Rohan. Without question, there are very serious problems in the world right now—people battling illness, others caught in the horrors of war. Each of us carries our own struggle. But I believe if you were called to face any of those situations, you would meet them just as you are facing this challenge before you right now. You haven't run. You've done everything within your power to understand what's happening and to move beyond it."

He leaned back in his chair, then continued, "Whether it's a great obstacle or a lesser one, what matters is that we meet it with our best effort. And right now, this—your panic attacks, depression, anxiety—is no small thing. These can rob someone of a good life if not addressed properly. We don't know what the future holds, but I believe everything you're learning here will strengthen your ability to face whatever lies ahead."

I swallowed and looked at him. "Calvin… what's gone so wrong in my life that I feel this broken?"

"Rohan, we all develop ways of dealing with conflict—habits and behaviors that help us get through life. But as we grow, what once worked can start to work against us. When that happens, we feel stress, confusion, even self-doubt."

He crossed his arms and sat back, "Our personalities are shaped from birth. You can't just slice off the parts you don't like and keep the rest. In fact, the very traits we wrestle with often shape the strengths we admire in ourselves. That's why it's so important to look closely at those uncomfortable parts—not to erase them, but to understand them. They're not flaws to be hidden; they're pieces of you that need attention, not shame."

I nodded, feeling it click. "So you're saying the parts of me I dislike won't disappear, but I can learn to recognize them—and keep them from running the show?"

"Precisely!" he said, leaning forward. "Rohan, we will never be perfect. We will always make mistakes and sometimes even behave in ways we wish we hadn't. That's part of being human. The goal is to know the many dimensions of who we are. This way we can modify our actions before they get past our attention. Adjust before acting. Mindfulness before regret."

I smiled and nodded in agreement. "I also really like the idea of not trying to be perfect," I said, surprised by how true it felt. "It's like taking off a heavy coat I didn't know I was wearing. There's something freeing in just being…human."

"You know what, Rohan? You may not realize it, but over the last few months, you've already been doing the work. What you've been doing, in the profession, is called activation therapy—taking deliberate action to feel better and get to know yourself. You sought help from your family doctor, and even if that path didn't feel right in the end, it was still a meaningful first step. Then you explored alternatives. You started practicing mindfulness meditation with Guruji, spent more time in nature, got back to exercise, and came here for therapy. That's initiative—and it's rare."

"Gosh, thanks, Calvin." I could feel my cheeks flush. "I just never know how to take compliments. I always feel like if people really knew me, they wouldn't have much good to say. Like I'm an imposter."

"That feeling comes from your own self-criticism. Everyone makes mistakes, but that doesn't erase their worth. Feeling ashamed of certain parts of yourself makes it harder when they show up. But if you bring those parts into the light, understand them, they lose their grip. Over time, you'll get to choose how you show up in the world. You're not here to erase parts of yourself, Rohan—you're here to understand them."

"Doesn't it make me fake if I'm hiding parts of myself?"

"We're not trying to hide them. I want you to meet the parts you've avoided. That's how you live in harmony with your whole self—instead of being haunted by the pieces you try to ignore."

"But how do I meet the parts I've been hiding? Sometimes I don't even know what I'm hiding. I just feel it when it takes over. Like we talked about before—judging others even though I don't want to. I know it comes from insecurity, but I just don't know where that insecurity started."

"We're complex beings. Sure, it helps to look back and get a sense of how we formed, but trying to pinpoint exactly when or why a trait developed can be a trap. We can spend years talking about our pain and still not change. That's why the goal is awareness—knowing the behaviours you want to work on and recognizing when they appear. Reflection matters, but real growth comes from action."

I chuckled. "That reminds me of something Guruji says, 'we confuse preparation for movement.' You can spend so much time planning that you forget to take the first step."

"Exactly. Now—last time, you mentioned a recurring dream. Would you be willing to share it with me?"

I paused to collect my thoughts. "I keep having the same dream, several times a week. I'm always deep, underground, far from anywhere familiar. The air feels suffocating, like something dreadful is about to happen. There's this constant sense that I'm supposed to be somewhere important. Every choice I make only seems to pull me further away. Most often I end up on a staircase, always descending. At the bottom I find a closed door that terrifies me. Without fail, I take another path instead—an alternate route that spares me the door but leads me farther from where I'm meant to go. The path is eerie but not frightening. Still, it leaves me frustrated, like I've betrayed myself. Every time I wake up from that dream, I feel exhausted… and anxious."

Dr. Hernandez took a slow breath and leaned back in his chair, his eyes drifting to the ceiling before settling on me again. "I wonder if the place you're meant to be…is behind that door. And every time you choose the other path, you're reinforcing the loop—avoiding the very thing that might hold some answers."

"Calvin, that door gives me the shivers even thinking about it when I'm awake. It radiates this dark, heavy energy."

Dr. Hernandez squinted, tilting his head, holding a friendly smirk. "Dark, you say? Dark like an abyss? The door may be terrifying in your dreams, but we can't take dreams at face value. Even if you recall it as frightening while awake, that doesn't mean what's behind it is equally so. It could simply be memories—or parts of your personality—you'd rather not face. And that's why we need to explore further. Something in you feels unsettled and is trying to surface."

He paused, letting the words settle. "Dreams often make things appear far worse, because they magnify our emotions. After all, dreams are constructed from the vastness of our subconscious—which is as boundless as the universe itself. With that much material to work with, it's no wonder dreams can get pretty creative."

Dr. Hernandez smiled and leaned forward. "Let's begin with the breathing exercise you've been practicing. Start with your eyes open, and as you feel more relaxed you can close them."

"I don't actually feel stressed right now." I said, unsure why he wanted me to use the technique. "Do you still want me to do it?"

He smiled again. "That's exactly why I want you to. You've got the perfect mindset to take us on a journey, Rohan."

"A journey?" I asked, feeling a little confused.

"Yes—a journey inside your mind. How about it?"

I smiled nervously. "Is this when you take me to meet the darkness? I'm ready, but a little worried."

He stood up, dimmed the lights, and partially closed the blinds until only a narrow sliver of daylight slipped through. Then he returned to his chair. "It's not like that at all, Rohan. You won't go anywhere you don't choose to. You're in charge, not me."

"Find a comfortable sitting position and take a few deep breaths."

I sat back into the cushion of the armchair and started my five second breathing technique: Five seconds in, five second hold, five seconds out. I continued and looked out the window at the swaying leaves of the oak tree just over Dr. Hernandez's shoulder. I thought of the majestic willow in the park and how this oak tree, too, had all of the beauty that she did. I recalled how Big Andy had said that trees were magical things. It was so true how we remember things differently when we're around trees. I slowly closed my eyes, breathing deeply—five seconds in, five second hold, five seconds out.

Dr. Hernandez spoke softly. "Keeping your eyes closed, and while breathing peacefully, I want you to follow my voice. Think of a place where you can go and be at peace. Maybe it's in the forest, or perhaps it's sitting in the park. Listen to the sounds around you. Feel the air on your skin. What are the smells that are there? Look around you. What else is there that captures your attention?"

I'm sitting beneath the willow, looking out over the pond. The leaves whisper in the warm spring breeze. The scent of blossoms lingers in the air, rich and alive. The willow shouldn't be here—not anymore—yet here she is, standing as majestic as ever. In the shallows, the white heron waits, still and graceful, like a sentinel. Watching. Aware.

She turns her head toward me, and speaks, and though her beak never moves, I hear her voice: "Rohan, look around and find a light. A warm and calming light."

The evening shrouds the park in darkness, as the sun offers its final glow. Streaks of orange and pink highlight the sky, low on the distant horizon. There, resting on the tip of the willow leaf, is a tiny blue butterfly. The dim rays of the setting sun gently touch its wings, causing it to illuminate with an otherworldly light. It takes flight, flying directly in front of me, and its glow fills the darkening park.

I can only see the shadows of the trees and the space being lit by the butterfly's gentle light. The heron fades into shadow, but her voice remains: "Take the peaceful light with you and keep it close. It will protect you. Feel its grounding force. Look around you, and find a door."

The soft blue light begins to drift down the gravel path, and I'm further calmed by the pleasant crunching sound beneath my feet. From the tall grass, countless blue sparks rise, floating upward like living stars. They settle in the branches, illuminating the canopy. Dew glimmers in their glow, as if the forest itself is breathing with quiet radiance.

Ahead, I see the outline of what looks like a garden shed. Big Andy is standing in front, raking the path leading to the front door. Beneath each window is a wooden flower box, each overflowing with white daisies and English Ivy. The door is cold steel, with a forbidding appearance. A stark contrast to the warmth of the woodshed, as though shielding something meant to stay hidden.

My chest tightens. My breath quickens. Big Andy turns, leaning on his rake, "Rohan, don't forget the light. You're not alone—I'm here if you need me."

He steps aside. "If you're ready, go on. Bring the peaceful light, and it will illuminate the way. It will keep you calm."

I stand before the steel door. It hums with more than memory. Behind it waits not just the past, but something far older—an eternal silence pressing against the noise of who I think I am.

The butterfly hovers before me, its glow steady. I breathe—five seconds in, five second hold, five seconds out. The door, familiar from countless dreams, yields easily beneath my hand. Darkness spills out. A staircase falls away into the abyss.

I step down. One stair. Then another. The butterfly's glow wraps around me, keeping fear at bay. The air rises damp and musty, carrying the scent of old cardboard boxes and forgotten years. From below, I hear a murmur—half child's voice, half sob— uncertain, haunting.

The dark thickens, pushing against the light, but the protective radiance holds.

Another voice echoes from everywhere and nowhere: "Breathe, you are not alone. Hold the light close."

I breathe—five seconds in, five second hold, five seconds out. As I exhale, the staircase opens into an immense space, utterly still. My light, stretched to its limits, reveals only emptiness—no ceiling, no walls. Just a lifeless hollow in the belly of the underworld. The floor is all that's visible. The darkness and light, play tricks on my eyes, making the floor surface appear to be more like a murky dark lake, shimmering like a black pearl, hiding its mysteries below the surface. This is in fact not a room at all—it's a place, not a physical place but something more. My deeper feelings—my intuition maybe—tell me that I could become lost here, trapped.

I can't hear the sounds of my footsteps or my breathing. I say, "hello," to see if I can hear the sound of my voice, but no words can be heard. With the complete absence of sound, I'm at least grateful for my glowing companion, the sole thread binding me to presence.

159

I can only describe this place as a threshold—a place between memory and the mystery beneath it, where thoughts go quiet not because they're answered, but because they're no longer needed.

My thoughts begin to feel hazy, dim, fading. I feel more and more disoriented. In that moment, Guruji's words echo through me: "Thoughts bring fear." In this place, thoughts hold no purpose. They only served to frighten, to tether me to the shape I have taken—the version of myself shaped by fear, not truth.

I close my eyes and breathe deeply, allowing calmness to empty my mind—five seconds in, five second hold, five seconds out. I feel weightless. Not able to feel the limits of my body, no sound —nothing— but it is not frightening. Opening my eyes I see the blue light from my companion grow brighter and brighter completely illuminating the abyss. It pulses once more, and in its glow, form begins to take shape—not from outside, but from within me. A memory, long sealed, floats to the surface.

With a sudden burst of light, I find myself in a familiar room, my mother is sitting on the edge of her bed weeping with her hands covering her face. I remember this.

"Mommy, it's going to be ok, I promise," a young voice says, from the crack in the partially opened door. I don't need to look, because I know who it is. The young boy pushes the door open a bit more and comes to sit next to his mother. He's not crying because he believes he must be strong—a kind little boy always searching for the right words to soothe. Able to help an

adult to find peace in the storm, yet terrified of the monsters under his bed.

"I'll always be here for you mommy, don't worry. Don't worry..."

The light flashes again.

Many years have gone by, and I'm at the beach with my father. I remember this day well. It's a splendid day and the last evening of a family vacation. My nineteenth birthday has just passed.

The sun is low on the horizon. My father turns to me, and begins to speak with such sadness: "You know Rohan, I don't talk much about the past, and you've never asked much either. I appreciate that. Some things we think we've moved on from, but we realize nothing we ever do is really gone. It just sits there inside of you, waiting. There're cracks in our armour Rohan, and the dark parts of us find those openings and come out of us in ways we wish they didn't. No wall or armour is thick enough to hold back the darkness, because it's not outside, it's right there inside with us. I brought a lot of my pains into our home, and for that I'm very sorry. You had to become a man far too fast, making up for my absence and bad temper. I've found my peace, and I know you'll find yours. Personal battles are inevitable, whether they be caused by physical war outside of us or a battle inside our own mind. Whatever pain we carry, life is our own path to walk, and no one can remove our problems but ourselves."

Leaning over, he pulls me close, telling me he loves me.

A voice finds me from far away, carried on the sea air: "I want you to take a deep breath and count backwards from five. When you reach one, I want you to open your eyes."

I don't question the voice. I begin to count. With each second, I'm pulled upward, back to breath, back to body. The armchair. The scent of mint. The steady hum of the room.

One.

I opened my eyes. Dr. Hernandez was sitting there with his kind smile, nodding his head with what looked like satisfaction. My mind was clear, but I felt somewhat disoriented.

"Take a moment, Rohan, and continue to breathe. You don't have to speak yet. Just let yourself come back fully," he said, leaning forward and offering me the tissue box.

To my surprise, tears had settled on my cheeks. I took a tissue, wiped my eyes, and continued to breathe. After a minute, the fog lifted, and my mind grew clear.

"I found the door, Calvin!" I said, with great excitement. "It really wasn't that scary. I don't know why my dreams make it so forbidding. Was I…was I hypnotized?"

Dr. Hernandez maintained his smile. "I would say it was more like a combination of hypnosis and meditation. You've made tremendous progress in a short time, Rohan. I knew you were ready."

"Ready for what?" I asked, still trying to ground myself.

"Ready to meet whatever was required of you to move forward. We just needed to trigger the right memory—something buried, something elusive—that your conscious mind had tucked away."

"Calvin, I have so many questions. It already feels like the place I visited is slipping away."

"You spoke out loud during much of the session, so I followed along. But we'll go over it together—it's not entirely clear to me what exactly happened."

I began recounting everything: the heron beneath the willow, the instruction to find a light, the warm presence of the butterfly. He nodded when I described the voice coming from the heron.

"That was me," he said. "You were translating my words into the imagery of your subconscious. The heron, the butterfly—these are meaningful symbols rising from within you to bridge our conversation with your internal journey."

"You're saying…when I heard your voice, I used images from my subconscious to stand in for you?"

"Exactly," he said. "At least in that particular moment. Please go on."

I told him about the glowing butterfly—how it looked exactly like the ones in Angelique's flower boxes—how it lit the way. Then, Big Andy's appearance outside the shed with the metal door, and how he reassured me before stepping inside.

"That was you too, wasn't it?" I was starting to understand the process a little better now.

Dr. Hernandez laughed softly. "Yes, that was me again. But from that point on, something different happened. You became very still. Your breathing slowed. Your face looked…serene."

Dr. Hernandez paused, eyes narrowing thoughtfully. "It wasn't quite what I expected. But since you showed no signs of distress, I let you continue. Sometimes, Rohan, when we cross a certain threshold, the mind steps aside—and something deeper takes over. That's what it felt like from my side."

"I never lingered long enough in the abyss to really know what it was," I continued, "but I'm pretty sure that's where I was when all went quiet."

Dr. Hernandez nodded. His eyes fixed on mine.

I paused to collect my thoughts, "Guruji's words came to me in the quiet of the darkness: 'thoughts bring fear'. In that moment I knew what I had to do. I breathed deeply and let go of my thoughts. Then suddenly the butterfly's glow transformed into pure light. It pushed back the darkness completely."

"My mother." I said, still disoriented. "Yes… that's right, I was talking to her. It was me—as a little boy—sitting beside her, trying to console her while she cried on the edge of her bed. I remember it so clearly. And yet…somehow I'd forgotten all about it. She'd had a big argument with my dad. Back then, their arguments were pretty common."

The words tumbled out faster than I could think—I was chasing the memory as it slowly slipped away—retreating back into the shadowed corners of my mind.

I continued, "My dad had stormed out of the house, and I heard her crying in her room. I remembered clinging to the hope I could help stop her tears."

The mask on the wall watched me— its face shaped like sorrow. "I hated seeing my father so frustrated and my mom so heartbroken."

165

I took a deep breath and went on, "They only quarrelled, and though it never escalated beyond that, it was still really stressful. My dad—he just couldn't talk. He'd get angry at simple things and my mom just didn't seem to know how to approach the whole thing."

"I didn't understand much back then, but I got good at sensing when a fight was about to start. I'd jump in, say just the right things, and act cheerful—anything to calm the room. It worked, at least on the surface."

There was a long pause. I steadied my voice and went on. "I remember telling her not to worry. I always told her not to worry. I got pretty good at cheering my mom up after those fights. Time went by and they got along better and better—hardly even argued after those earlier years. People would even say they were like the perfect couple—inseparable and best of friends. They were right." I pushed back the tears.

Dr. Hernandez leaned forward in his chair, "It looks like it upsets you to talk about those days. You learned at a very young age that you could take away some of your mom's pain. You told her she didn't have to worry—maybe even leave the worrying up to you?"

"I guess I spent an abnormal amount of time running through every scenario that might unfold, when my dad would be in one of his moods. I became quite the ruminator, as you'd say."

There was a long silence as I glanced back at the masks on the wall, thinking of how many emotions we carry. Most of us move through life and never really know why we feel what we feel. We think emotions just happen to us, but they're a part of us—and we can come to know them better than we realize. Some are darker, and when they rise, we convince ourselves the enemy is outside, blaming the world for how we feel…when all along it's hiding in us.

"My dad!" I said out loud as the memories of the experience flickered "I also saw my dad, Calvin. It was a family vacation at the beach, and I was with him. It was the first time he ever acknowledged the tensions that he brought into the house. I remembered that day so well too. By that time in our lives, the fighting in the house had stopped for a good number of years. He and I were actually starting to spend a lot more time together. He started taking an interest in the things I had found that made me happy. He really did change, and I never knew why or how. It's like he flipped a switch and became super calm and easy going. It's funny but I was never actually angry at my dad—he was my hero in a lot of ways. I really love both my mom and dad and always did. They just had struggles but eventually everyone found some peace."

"Everyone?" Dr. Hernandez said, gently tilting his head to one side.

"I guess, not everyone. I'd go to school and be really disruptive. I couldn't stay still in class, and getting sent to the principal's office was a regular occurrence. Funny, on parents' night at the school, the teachers would tell my mom and dad that I was a nice kid, but I just couldn't pay attention, and I'd distract the other kids."

Dr. Hernandez was nodding in acknowledgment. "How long did that go on for?"

"By the time I got into high school my study habits just weren't well established. Every year, I was more and more behind, until it got to the point where I would just barely make it through each year. Come college, my bad study habits and disorganized way of doing things just didn't cut it. I chose programs that weren't as demanding but I would also struggle through them. I never found what it was that I could excel in during my college years."

"Does some of this have to do with why you've said that you sometimes feel ashamed of how you're turning out in life?"

"People around me just seem to have things more figured out than I do. I've felt many times like I'm missing out. Others are getting ahead, and I'm trapped in my stress and anxiety."

Dr. Hernandez nodded attentively, then said, "Maybe it's that feeling—thinking others seem to have it all figured out—that triggers the judging part of you. I stress the word 'seem', Rohan, because no one really has it all together. But when we're struggling, it's easy to idealize other people's lives. Truth is, we're all just trying to make sense of this world in our own way."

I nodded. "I'm beginning to see that more clearly, Calvin. I've heard it again and again—even from my dad that day on the beach—that we have to walk our own path. We can't walk other people's path, and they can't walk ours. I just need to shake this feeling of failure. Don't get me wrong—I read, I learn, I open myself to things that help me grow. And still, no matter what I do, it's like I'm always looking over my shoulder…haunted by my screwups."

Dr. Hernandez stood, pulled opened the blinds, and let the light back into the room. Then he sat down. "So it feels like a shadow haunting you—like no matter what you do, you can't quite get to where you want to go?"

"Exactly. I've said it many times—I feel shy and ashamed talking about my failures. No matter how much I succeed at other things, I'm always trying to avoid messing up again, or worrying that something bad will happen and add to the list. There's just something about failure that drags me down. Not just sadness—it feels heavier, like it could trigger something really bad. It's hard to explain."

Dr. Hernandez sat back in his chair, interlocked his fingers, and placed his palms on his chest. "When we live in turbulent homes, adopting a role as peacemaker can be detrimental to us. Children can't always succeed at creating peace in an adult world. I'm sure there were times when you wouldn't succeed in stopping the arguments. Seeing your mom cry could make you feel like you had failed. You would think that you had to try even harder the next time, and would try to think of all the ways the fight would go down. You would begin to ruminate about possible scenarios and solutions. A ruminating child—and a ruminating adult for that matter—is someone highly susceptible to experiencing depression and anxiety. Do you feel like it's possible that you learned to feel responsible for other people's happiness? Maybe, when you slip up that makes the people important to you unhappy?"

"There's definitely something to that. It feels like it has something to do with feeling that I need to hide who I really am. When I had to put on that act to make everyone happy, it's like I got used to putting myself aside in order to be what others needed me to be. I'm often trying so hard to make up for my shortcomings that I lose track of who I want to actually be. Life stops making sense when you're stuck living through the lens of who you think others want you to be."

"What do you think other people see when they look at you through that lens?"

I hated looking weak and vulnerable, but my eyes teared up. "They see me as not what they hoped for—that I let them down." I looked over Dr. Hernandez's shoulder at the quiet oak tree. "I think that's why I like sitting in the park, breathing and being quiet. There's no judgement there. Just being. I'd like to be able to feel that way when I'm around others and not just when I'm in the park."

"You know Rohan, we can't be everything to everyone. We can only be our best selves—and even that takes time, practice, and exploration. I'll remind you again: we're not perfect. We make mistakes, and we'll make them again. I think we need to help you to change the lens through which you look at yourself. I don't believe for a second people see you the way you imagine they do."

He sat forward, both hands on his lap. "Let's pick up here in a few days. In the meantime, give yourself some space—clear your mind with some exercise and meditation. And remember: you couldn't be the solution for your mom and dad. That was theirs to find. In the end, you can't walk someone else's path. Keep reminding yourself of this, Rohan: you can't change people. You can only work to change yourself. You're doing great, Rohan. I'm proud of you."

We arranged our next appointment, and I left his office still feeling a bit hazy, but also feeling hopeful that my life was changing for the better.

A Meeting of Souls

Then Jesus spoke to them again, saying, "I am the light of the world. He who follows me shall not walk in darkness, but have the light of life.

—John 8:12

Emerson Street was only about a twenty-minute walk, and the day was still glorious, so I started on my way. The neighbourhood around Dr. Hernandez's office was very quiet, with only a scattering of people about.

I crossed the street to glance at the tapestry of Lord Ganesha, displayed in the storefront window. The price tag was pinned to the bottom right corner—well beyond my budget. I chuckled, amused at the irony: I couldn't afford a depiction of the remover of obstacles...because of an obstacle. I paused, imagining it hanging in my sitting area. I usually kept the space bare—clutter made my mind feel heavy. But maybe this was a small nudge, a sign to start envisioning something new. I'd worked hard for the sanctuary I called home. Maybe, in time, this tapestry would find its place there too.

As I continued walking, my thoughts drifted back to my session with Dr. Hernandez. He truly had a gift—guiding me straight to the heart of what I needed to face. The door, the staircase, the darkness…it was all so precise.

My mother, sitting on the edge of the bed, was crystal clear in my mind. So was my father on the beach—his voice, his words. I thought about how, as a young boy, I had learned to use words like tools—gentle instruments to calm storms between my parents, especially to soothe my mother's tears. For a child, it had felt powerful… magical, even. All I had wanted was peace in the house—for her, for him, and for me. They seemed to have found theirs. I, on the other hand, had clearly taken a different path.

The walk was peaceful and helped to clear my mind. I realized I was close to my destination. I hadn't been to this part of the city in years, but it was as I remembered—old, dignified, and draped in history. Massive trees lined every property. Towering oaks, ash, and silver maples stretched their limbs skyward, their roots nestled in front yards of homes built a century or two ago. Spring flowers were in abundance—yellow and red tulips, white daisies, and daffodils—lining the walkways like nature's welcome mats. Creeping purple phlox spilled over garden stones, and the air was fragrant with that unmistakable scent of spring.

I arrived at the corner of Emerson Street and made my way up the narrow road that came to a steep ascent. The canopies overhead created a cathedral of green, breathtaking in their majesty.

But my awe quickly gave way to confusion—and then a jolt of unease. The address I'd come to find was little more than the charred skeleton of a house. Boarded up. Scorched stone walls. A roof mostly caved in. The window frames were blackened, their glass long gone. Whatever had happened here was not that recent, but the ruin still carried a kind of solemn weight.

I stood motionless, trying to process what I was seeing. Could this really be the place Guruji once called home? From the look of it, it had once been a grand residence.

Just to be sure, I pulled the folded paper from my pocket and checked the address again. The numbers matched. The scorched metal door plate left no doubt.

I heard a shuffle behind me and turned to see an elderly man approaching. He had a thick crown of snow-white hair and a matching mustache set against a fair complexion. Slim and upright in a light blue sweater and faded blue jeans, he moved with quiet grace. I guessed he was in his late seventies, but his perfect posture and steady stride made it hard to know for sure.

With a kind smile and bright green eyes that held both warmth and knowingness, he spoke in a soft but confident tone. I felt an immediate connection to him.

"Sad sight to see, isn't it?" he said, glancing at the paper in my hand and then toward the charred remnants of the house. "Do you know Guruji?" he asked, turning back to meet my eyes.

A ripple of emotion moved through me. I felt unsettled, unsure what he was about to tell me.

"I do," I said. "I've only known him a short time, less than a week—but he's changed my life in a way I'll never be able to repay."

The man looked down at the sidewalk and smiled, though his eyes were glazed with a quiet sorrow. "Anyone who's met Guruji says the same. He was my neighbor for the better part of twenty years. Came all the way from India, sold everything he owned just to bring his message of peace and spirit here." He gestured gently to the burned ruins. "This was his ashram. Hundreds of us came here over the years. A place of light. A sanctuary."

He paused, squinting toward the blackened stone archway, then added, "He's no ordinary man, you know. Some of his students still see him— though from what I hear, only the newest ones. He said he had to remain available to those in the greatest need. He also told us that we already had everything we needed. That our journey now is in the doing, not the talking. To seek his presence again, he said, would be to cling to what is impermanent. We must each walk our own path now."

I smiled. "That sounds exactly like him." I looked over at the burnt home, "When did the fire happen?"

"A little over a year ago," he said, rubbing the back of his neck. "It moved fast. Thank God no one was home. He lost nearly everything. A few things were salvaged, taken to his new place. But if you'd seen him afterward… calm as a lake. Anyone else would've been devastated. But Guruji just smiled. Said wealth and possessions are part of life's dance—but never to be clung to. That our attachment to what we build is the seed of our suffering. So much of life's plan is beyond our control."

"That's Guruji, alright," I said with a small laugh. "I'm Rohan, by the way." I extended my hand.

"Walter," he said, taking my hand firmly in both of his. "Pleased to meet you, Rohan."

I asked, "Were you a student of Guruji as well?"

Walter gave a slow nod, his face softening. "I was, and he changed my life more than I can put into words. When he first moved in, I watched people come and go. At the time, my wife and I were nearing retirement—we had lots of plans. A few months later, she fell ill—something sudden, aggressive. We never had time to understand it, let alone prepare. Within three months…she was gone."

Walter's eyes began to well with tears. He sniffed and looked away. "I wanted to meet Guruji. I truly did. But I was conflicted. I was a pastor—I'd devoted my life to the teachings of Christ, and I wasn't sure if seeking wisdom from a Hindu teacher would betray my faith. I was torn. But the truth is, my struggle wasn't really about religion. It was that I felt betrayed by life itself. My faith had been shaken to the core."

He looked up, eyes bright with memory. "One evening, deep in the fog of grief, I walked up to his door and knocked. He welcomed me as if I'd been expected all along. We sat in his solarium— the back room with its walls of glass—delicate rays of the setting sun brushing the sky with pinks and purples. It's so vivid in my mind…I just broke. Everything spilled out. And what he gave me in return was silence. Stillness. And a way to breathe."

Walter chuckled softly, almost sheepish. "It felt like prayer—but deeper. Not words to God, but a dissolving into something vast. I don't know if I was dreaming, or if he was guiding something ancient—something sacred. All I know is, I slipped out of myself. My body vanished. My thoughts ceased. And in that stillness, I heard a message. I can't say from where—but I believe it was from God. And in that moment, I knew that everything was as it was meant to be."

He kicked lightly at a twig on the sidewalk. "I never asked Guruji what he did. Maybe I didn't want to seem foolish—or maybe I was afraid too much talk would steal the magic. Either way, afterward, I saw life differently. He told me that the journey inward is about emptying the mind— releasing the chatter, the clinging, the identity. Returning to what we really are. And he said, such things can't be explained. Not with words. Words are born of thought. And where we were—there were no thoughts."

I nodded, the memory of Guruji's words echoing. "He said something similar—that *thoughts bring fear*. He's been guiding me to sit quietly in the darker corners of my mind. And when I really go still—the fear fades, and something older than thought begins to rise."

Walter's eyes lit with recognition. "We live in a world obsessed with thinking—intellect, logic, reason. None of that leads to the soul. If anything, it only deepens our disconnection. What Guruji gave me wasn't knowledge—it was remembering. The kind that happens in silence."

179

He smiled gently. "That day changed everything. I became a better person, a better pastor. Softer. My sermons turned into prayers rather than speeches. People said they could feel something in the room—an energy, a presence—when we gathered. And I knew it wasn't me. I was only the instrument. The message came through me, not from me."

He caught himself and blushed. "Sorry, I've gone on too long. But when someone says Guruji changed their life…I get carried away."

"Don't apologize," I said. "I get it. I really do. Has Guruji said anything about rebuilding?"

Walter sighed. "Delays, mostly. Insurance headaches, heritage restrictions…the usual mess. Funny, isn't it? Guruji might be a transcendent soul, but even he has to wrestle with contractors and city permits." He chuckled softly, then shook his head—seriousness returning to his face, "I imagine this will take at least another year."

"Well, I hope it gets rebuilt someday. And I hope we meet again, Walter."

I extended my hand. He clasped it again, warmly.

Walter patted my shoulder, and said, "I can see you walk in the light, young man. Be well. And please—tell Guruji I send my love and gratitude."

We both turned to part ways, but Walter paused and called back with a mischievous glint in his eye. "Hey, Rohan…do you think this was a sign? Meeting like this? I wasn't even supposed to be home today."

His mustache curled with a grin.

I grinned back. "If two fellow journeymen randomly meet and share stories about a man who saved their lives…yeah, I'd say we just saw one."

We both laughed, and as I walked away, I felt the light inside me grow brighter.

Drawn By An Inner Voice

"When you look at trees, you allow them. You understand why one is bent, or turned, or different. You appreciate the tree. The minute you get near humans, you lose all that. That judgment mind comes in. And so, I practice turning people into trees."

—Ram Dass

I arrived home around 4:30 p.m. and made a light bite to eat before my run. While the kettle boiled, I drank two big glasses of water. Then I carried my tea out onto the back balcony. The breeze was warm. The clouds drifted like cotton across the sky, and the sun was low on the horizon.

Something inside me stirred.

After what I'd seen in my journey with Dr. Hernandez—the willow, the door, the dark—I knew exactly where I needed to run. It wasn't just for exercise this time. The pull was quiet but certain.

I finished my drink, changed into shorts and a T-shirt, and stepped out onto the sidewalk, starting at a gentle pace.

I passed Angelique's shop—she was talking to a delivery man, so I continued without pause.

The sky was an artist's dream—hues of pink, gold, and soft orange poured across the horizon, spilling into the treetops that lined the street. Billowy white clouds, darkened silver underneath, gave the illusion of a painted sky.

Light would last for another hour—just enough.

By the time I reached the park, I had slowed to a walk. The city fell behind. Meadow grass replaced asphalt and pavement. Spring flowers bursting in yellow, red, and violet bathed in the last rays of the sun. Frogs chirped from the pond, joining the birds in a kind of twilight chorus.

As I made my way to the center of the park, once again in awe of the great trees, I thought about Big Andy. He said trees are the closest to God he gets to in a day. I had to agree. This park had become my sanctuary. These trees, quiet as monks, had listened to my pain, asking nothing in return. They didn't answer—they didn't need to. With trees, we're not expected to be anything. And maybe that's why their presence feels like prayer—in stillness.

I had just arrived at the giant willow branch and sat for a brief moment to begin my breathing exercises, when a small utility vehicle rumbled up beside me. I was happy to see it was Big Andy driving, and in the back of his truck bed, were four saplings with burlap wrappings around their huge root bulbs. I waved to him as he stopped, but he left the motor running.

"Hey there, Rohan," he said, with a broad grin. He looked comically large inside the tiny cab—like a gentle giant stuffed into a child's toy truck.

"Planting more trees, Big Andy?" I asked, nodding toward the contents of the cargo bed.

"These fellas're going in the ground tomorrow. It's almost dark so I'm just going to drop'em off on the other side of the park where the new section's being prepped. It's where they'll start their new life. Hop on in, if you've got a few minutes…I'll show you the new section of the park—it hasn't been open to the public in over a year."

"I'd love that, Big Andy," I said, already curious. I'd passed that boarded-off area a few times lately. You could see all the tops of the big trees, but not so much as a glimpse of the grounds area underneath them.

I climbed in the passenger seat and off we went.

Andy spoke but didn't take his eyes off of the path as there were a number of people strolling about, enjoying the splendid evening.

"This is the last run—I've been back and forth all day," he said. "I'm short two workers, so it's just me tonight—still chipping away."

We reached the closed section of the park. The plywood barrier stretched on for at least a city block in each direction. Big Andy stopped at a gated entry, screening off what lay behind, from view. He climbed out, unlocked a large chain and swung open the gate, with practiced ease. Once in, he quickly locked up behind us, and we were on our way.

"As you can see, there's still a bit of work to do but we're getting there," Big Andy said as I looked about in amazement.

We drove along the new gravel path that wound through the rolling hills of the park. Tall trees stood like guards, their leafy canopies ready to offer shade from the coming summer heat. Beneath them, beds of young perennial flowers and shrubs had begun to settle into the earth. The meadow grasses swayed lush and green, their blades catching the last golden light. As we passed clusters of foxtail lilies and lupins, tiny blue butterflies scattered like sky-colored confetti in the fading sun.

I looked over at Big Andy and smiled.

He hollered over the growl of the engine, "As close to God as you'll ever get." He gave a satisfied nod—his face lit with quiet contentment.

185

We came to a clearing where more than thirty saplings lay neatly side by side, their roots bundled in damp burlap, awaiting their moment to go into the soil. The sight stirred something warm in me—a gentle happiness, like watching a future being gently set in motion.

Big Andy climbed out. "We're building a zone of wild diversity," he said, sweeping his arm across the landscape. "Variety of trees, shrubs, perennials—the works. A haven for bees, birds, butterflies…and folks who aren't afraid to get their feet wet and their shoes dirty."

He dropped the tailgate.

"Let me give you a hand with those," I offered, walking to the back of the truck.

"I won't say no," he chuckled. "Been a long day, and being short-handed, it's catching up with the old body." He put his hands on the small of his back and leaned back with a groan. Something popped.

"What happened to the crew?" I asked, trying not to pry, as I gently lifted one of the saplings. "Nice dogwood," I added, setting it down beside the truck.

Big Andy raised an eyebrow. "Had to let 'em go. No passion for the dirt. But you…you really know your trees. Most folks wouldn't call a dogwood by name."

186

I grinned as I reached for the next one. "My uncle used to own a nursery. I worked summers there through high school. Never told him, but I would've done it for free."

We both laughed.

"I'd open the place before sunrise," I said, while setting the sapling down gently on its side. "My friends hated the mornings, but it was my favorite time of the day. I'd ride my bike in the quiet while the city slept. When I arrived in the parking lot, that crunch of gravel under my tires, in the stillness—it was magic. That sound still lives with me to this day. I'd walk the grounds on my morning inspection—the shrubs, trees, and rafters of the pergolas—all alive with birdsong. The greenhouses were like temples. Peaceful. Sacred."

Big Andy listened without saying a word.

I took a deep refreshing breath. "The people would walk in and just…light up," I went on. "There's something special about buying a tree. It's not like buying some commodity or some junk you just don't need. When someone picked a tree, their eyes lit up. And if we told them we could deliver it that same day? Pure joy."

I paused, resting the last tree on the grass. "I miss seeing that look in people's eyes."

Big Andy nodded, something shifting in his gaze.

187

I couldn't stop expressing my memories. "My uncle taught me everything. I was his apprentice for over four years. I wanted to study landscape architecture, but my science grades weren't strong enough, and I didn't have the discipline to turn it around. My uncle…he passed. Suddenly. I was nearly nineteen. After that, my aunt sold the nursery."

I looked out at the saplings.

"The new owners turned it into one of those big home improvement stores, with the garden section tacked on like an afterthought. They had their own hiring system, and I wasn't interested. They paved over the old gravel parking lot…"

Big Andy didn't say a word at first. He just looked at me like he was seeing something new. A seed he hadn't noticed was already planted.

He finally spoke. "Thanks for the help, Rohan. Much appreciated. Hop back in and I'll take you to the other side of the park."

The ride back was slower, now that darkness had blanketed the grounds. The headlights swept across the gravel path, now empty of people. Every so often, the beams would catch a glint of tiny eyes watching from the shadows—the park's nocturnal residents stirring to life.

"What kind of work do you do now, Rohan?" Big Andy asked, breaking the stillness of the drive.

"I'm between jobs, actually. Starting a new one in a couple of weeks. Though…if I'm honest, I'm not exactly looking forward to it." The old worry stirred again—that tug of trying to build peace within a life that no longer fit. I heard Angelique's words echoed in my mind: *Your peace will come when your duties and your spirit begin to walk together.*

Big Andy gave my thigh a friendly punch. Pulling me from my thoughts. "If you ever feel that job's not for you, just let me know. I've got two openings, and you already seem to have most of the know-how."

I glanced at him, surprised—maybe even stunned.

"Just think on it, Rohan. You'd only need a bit of mentoring on the particulars here, but truthfully—you've got more real experience than half my crew. Those summers apprenticing under your uncle? Hell, you're damn near a certified journeyman already. What matters most is the heart, and you've got that. I do all the hiring, and final say's mine. Benefits are solid, pay's among the best in the state. And this park—isn't your average patch of grass. It's closer to a forest than a city park. You'll learn plenty and never be bored. City even

189

pays for courses tied to the work—so who knows? Maybe that degree's still in the cards after all. But don't say anything now. Take a few days. I'll keep holding down the fort till I find the right people."

We arrived back at the main path. I hopped out.

"Thanks again, Big Andy— for the tour and the offer. Honestly, I hadn't realized how valuable that old knowledge was until you pointed it out. I'll definitely be in touch soon."

"No rush, Rohan. There's something about you—from the day we met—something told me we crossed paths for a reason. Maybe we're figuring that out together. Appreciate the muscle, too— might've saved my back." He laughed, then added as he began to pull away, "You know, back in the old country, we say your name, 'Rowan.' The Rowan tree—tree of life, they call it. Never forget, lad, sometimes a name holds more than you think."

I watched the taillights vanish into the trees, and I turned toward home.

I jogged back, arriving around 8:00 p.m. After a light dinner, I made a cup of tea and sat out on the front steps. The night sky was clear. Even this close to the city, the stars shone through the gaps in the clouds, steady and bright above the glow of neighbouring buildings.

There was a lot to reflect on.

My session with Dr. Hernandez had unearthed something long buried—memories I hadn't consciously forgotten, but hadn't known how to face. His words echoed: *"When we live in turbulent homes, adopting a role as peacemaker can be detrimental to us. Children can't always succeed at creating peace in an adult world."* We can't take on other people's pain. We can walk beside them, but they have to face their own path.

I thought of Walter—Guruji's home. All of his things reduced to ashes—and yet, in the midst of that loss, he still opened his space to me. He never asked for payment. He said, "Pay what you can." Guruji didn't chase anything, prosperity found him, because his spirit and his duties walked together. He simply showed up—still, silent, and generous. He was no ordinary man.

I sipped the last of my tea and stepped back inside. Tomorrow would come, and with it, a decision to make.

Big Andy's offer stirred something I hadn't felt in years. I remembered that final day at my uncle's nursery. I hadn't realized how deeply I missed it—the early mornings, physical work, the scent of soil and pine, the quiet dignity of the trees. Something in me was waking again. I wasn't sure where it would lead—but for the first time in a long while, I was excited to find out.

Full Circle

There is only one way to learn... It's through action. Everything you need to know you have learned through your journey.

—Paulo Coelho, The Alchemist

I awoke well before sunrise. My watch read 5:25 a.m. In the quiet stillness of the morning, I walked to the kitchen, drank a tall glass of water, and put the kettle on. I lit a stick of sandalwood and stood for a moment, watching its thin spiral rise and dissolve into the dim light. It was raining outside— a soft, steady rain.

I changed into sweats and did my morning exercises indoors. The squats and push-ups came easier than before—my body moved steady, fluid, almost weightless. I realized I'd have to increase the repetitions.

It wasn't until I'd finished that I noticed something deeper—my head was completely clear. No brain fog. No side effects. Just a centered presence. My body truly was coming back into balance, just as Guruji had told me in our very first meeting.

I returned to the sitting area and lowered myself onto the cushion in the center of the room. No wall behind me. No need. I sat cross-legged and upright, a quiet sense of accomplishment flickering in my chest. I closed my eyes and began my five-second breathing sequence, allowing each inhale and exhale to pull me deeper into stillness. Thoughts faded into background mist.

Then the phone rang.

It startled me. The sound felt intrusive in the sacred silence of morning. I answered—it was my mother.

"Rohan," she said, her voice trembling. "It's your father. It doesn't look good. We're at the General Hospital—he's in emergency."

I stood up quickly. "What happened, mom?" My legs felt hollow beneath me.

"He was in the back room…I heard a loud bang. He fell. I don't know why. He's conscious now, but…disoriented. He doesn't remember what happened."

"I'll be right there. Tell dad I'm on my way."

Fortunately, I was already dressed. I slipped on my sneakers and headed out the door. There was a taxi stand a few blocks up. I ran, my thoughts spiraling: would he be alive by the time I got there? Mom said he was awake…disoriented, yes, but still conscious. Was that a good sign? I didn't know. I just ran.

The drizzle had stopped, and as I turned the corner, the sun broke over the horizon. The sky exploded into shades of orange, crimson, and rose. The wet pavement shimmered like a mirror, catching the colors of the sky.

I inhaled deeply, a steady breath. Please, I whispered inwardly, let me see him before it's too late.

I reached the taxi stand. A line of cabs waited in the final moments of morning silence. I knocked on the back window of the first one.

"I need to get to the General Hospital. Emergency entrance," I said, as I slid into the back seat, still catching my breath.

Thankfully, morning traffic hadn't begun, so the drive flowed smoothly. A few minutes in, we stopped at the red light in front of Angelique's shop. She was already outside, earlier than usual, setting up her display racks. Her white hair was tied back with a bright yellow headband, and she wore a flowing summer dress—green and white with swirls of yellow and blue butterflies, appearing to flutter as she moved.

She was close enough to the cab that I rolled down the window and called out her name. I just needed to see her smile.

She turned instantly, that radiant face lighting up at the sound of my voice. We were the only car stopped at the light.

"Not on foot or bike this morning, Rohan?" she teased, her smile wide.

That smile—there was something about it. It carried the kind of reassurance that reminded you everything would be all right, no matter what the world brought. It didn't deny pain—it just refused to let it win.

"I'll see you later, Angelique," I said, the words tumbling out before I could think. "I'm on my way to the hospital. My father…it's not looking good."

Something inside me needed to tell her— not for sympathy, but because I was learning that while I alone must walk my path, I didn't have to walk it in isolation. There was strength in letting someone walk beside me.

Her smile softened into something deeper—steady, knowing.

"I'll be here," she said. She brought both hands together in prayer, then blew a kiss and touched her heart.

195

Though her smile faltered slightly, the light in her eyes remained. Something about her made me think of Walter—how he said that Guruji had helped him understand that everything was as it should be. I felt a small but powerful wave of solace pass through me. Not a blind optimism—something more grounded. A recognition that life would unfold as it must. I couldn't control everything, but I could control my response. My own actions. There was unexpected comfort in that. Maybe even freedom.

The light changed and we pulled away.

I sat forward in the seat, watching the road through the windshield. Tucked under the passenger-side sun visor was a small picture card. A printed image of the Buddha, with a quote beneath it. I leaned closer and read the words aloud, but in a whisper: "*No one saves us but ourselves. No one can and no one may. We ourselves must walk the path*"—The Buddha.

I exhaled and leaned back into the seat, letting the truth of it settle into me. The driver glanced at me in the rear-view mirror, meeting my eyes with gentle compassion. Then he looked toward the quote on the visor and gave the smallest of nods, as if to say, yes… that one matters.

I closed my eyes halfway and let my breath deepen. Silence returned, the cab moving softly through the early city light.

We passed the east side of the park. The dense trees and shrubs lined the road like a living wall—an untamed boundary between the noise of the city and the silence of nature. I pictured Big Andy already there, placing new saplings into the earth.

After a few minutes, the park was behind us. We passed the corner where the Bliss Centre stood. I looked up at the third-floor window where Guruji had opened his temporary sanctuary. It had been less than two weeks, since I walked through his door, broken and uncertain. That single meeting had altered the course of my life. His tragedy—losing his home—had brought him here. And through it, to me. Life is a mystical journey—full of improbable, yet life-defining encounters. I took a deep breath in reverence to my mentor.

Soon, we pulled up to the emergency entrance of the hospital. I handed the fare over the seat and thanked the driver. As I opened the door to get out, he rolled down his window and called to me.

"Please," he said, handing the card from the sun-visor to me, "take it."

I looked at the card again: *No one saves us but ourselves. No one can and no one may. We ourselves must walk the path*—The Buddha.

I nodded, deeply grateful.

As he pulled away, he leaned out once more and called softly, "Peace be with you, my friend."

I turned quickly and trotted toward the emergency entrance. Overhead, the familiar brick smokestack loomed from the center of the hospital. I never thought I'd be back here under these circumstances.

The sliding glass doors parted, and I stepped into a flurry of motion—corridors alive with movement. Hospital staff hurried past, pushing equipment, reading charts, answering pagers. Voices called out across stations, some urgent, others routine, all of them layered over the rhythmic chorus of beeping machines and distant intercom calls. It was organized chaos—unrelenting.

Down the hallway, I saw my mother standing in a doorway, her small figure dwarfed by the bustle around her. I approached and gently placed my hand on her shoulder. She turned to face me, and her tears came immediately. I wrapped her in my arms. She pressed her face against my shoulder, her body shaking. She felt so small.

I could recall the days when she towered above me. Time had crept in quietly and carved itself into her.

I looked past her into the room. My father lay still in the bed, eyes closed, IV lines in both arms, monitors blinking behind his head.

"He's stable, Rohan," my mother said. "The doctor said they'll have more information soon. They're running some tests."

She sat at the foot of the bed. I walked to the other side and took my father's hand. His eyes fluttered open, and he smiled weakly.

"Rohan, my boy…I'm sorry for all this fuss," he said, his voice low but clear. "One minute I was up, the next, I'm down, and in an ambulance."

"Just rest, dad," I said, squeezing his hand. "Don't waste energy apologizing."

I glanced back at my mother. She sat hunched over, dabbing her eyes with a tissue. I moved beside her, placed an arm around her shoulder, and patted my father's leg with the other hand.

I wanted to say, don't worry, but it didn't feel right. Of course she was worried. Words like that can't erase the ache in someone's heart.

"You know I'm here for you both," I said, instead. "I love you. Whatever you need—I'm here. Let's just wait to hear what the doctor says."

They both looked tired, aged in ways I hadn't noticed before. I remembered my father when he could carry me on his shoulders, when he ran alongside my bike, cheering me on as I learned to ride. I remembered my mother trying to balance on my skateboard in the driveway, laughing as she almost fell. No fear. No fragility. Their bodies were different now—but the love remained.

My father's eyes studied us quietly, a soft pride in his gaze. "You know, Rohan," he said, "I've watched you comfort your mother more times than I can count. You've talked sense into this old fool more than once or twice as well." He chuckled, then his eyes welled up. "You've always looked out for everyone—and just about everything's wellbeing. Even as a boy, you brought home bugs, birds, and a whole sort of stray creatures. Anything hurt, you had to heal."

A memory flashed across his face.

"Remember the seagull?" he asked, his voice thick with emotion. "The one that hurt its wing?"

I smiled. "I remember."

"You tied up his wings—told us it was a temporary splint—and kept him in your room for a week. You made these little bowls to feed him. Then you made me drive you to that parking lot behind all those fast-food joints. You said it was the best place because of all the French fries people dropped."

We both laughed. "When you took him out of the box and let him go…Rohan, your face—I'll never forget it. He opened his wings and soared into the sky like he'd never been hurt. You jumped and shouted, said you could feel the wind off his wings hit your face. You were so full of joy."

He paused, holding my gaze. "That day changed me."

I was silent. My throat tightened.

"I remember thinking—why does it matter? One gull, in a world of gulls. But I got it. Saving him wasn't about changing the world. It was about bringing meaning to your own life. And you did. Watching you helped me realize that the world doesn't give us meaning—we give meaning to the world. You showed me that, Rohan. You helped me start down my own path. A healing path."

I listened closely. I had never heard my father speak this way—except that one day on the beach during our family vacation. As he got older, he was always friendly and easy to be around, but very quiet, only spoke if there was something that needed saying.

"All that bickering back then…" he sighed. "I know it wasn't easy for you, and I'm not saying it didn't leave a mark. Your mother and I—we were far from perfect. If I could go back and do things differently, I would. But Rohan, even so, I've always believed that part of you—the part that needed to care, to make peace—was already there. It wasn't something we put into you. If anything, we made it harder. But that need in you…it came from deep inside. And sooner or later, you were always going to come face-to-face with it."

He looked at me with quiet honesty. "You've got a heart that wants to mend things. And hearts like that don't stay quiet forever. Whether you grew up in chaos or calm, I think you'd still have to walk this path—this path of learning to live with the weight of feeling everything so deeply."

He smiled gently. "But don't think I ever saw you as soft. You've always had fire in you. You stood up for people—didn't matter how big the bully. And you never looked for someone to blame your troubles on. Even when it would have been the easier path."

"How come you never told me any of this before, Dad?" I asked. "About your discovery— your healing path? What you thought about my struggles?"

"You got busy, Rohan. You were often on the go and your visits were short. To be honest, you seemed distracted and preoccupied—kind of like you weren't in the moment. Your mother and I wanted to give you your space. It was tough watching you. That look of excitement you had in your younger years seemed to fade. We all get older, and it's not a judgement, just an observation. But let me tell you—just ten minutes ago, I was lying in this bed feeling like a shadow was pressing down on me. Then I opened my eyes and saw you standing there, it was like the light had returned in you. In that instant, I felt something lift off of me—like my strength came rushing back."

I was about to respond when the doctor came in.

"We've got what looks like good news," he said. "All tests came back clear. I'd say the fall was from a sudden drop in blood pressure—nothing more serious than that. We're going to keep you for observation overnight, but as of now, everything looks good. You're rehydrated, and vitals are strong."

The doctor turned to my mom and me with a smile. "Doesn't always happen that I get to deliver good news. When it does, I take it as a reminder—fresh starts are possible at any age. I'll leave you alone now, and get some rest, all of you."

After he left, my mom embraced my father. Their tears mixed with quiet relief. She looked over at me with the same smile I always tried so hard to bring out in her. I loved that smile. Even in the worst of times, she had a way of shining light.

I was grateful that I had helped her through the years, even if it meant carrying some of her burdens along the way. Like my father said, maybe that was just my nature. Dr. Hernandez was helping me to see that all parts of myself had value—even the ones that were heavy. They didn't need to be buried. They just needed to be understood.

"I can't do much here right now," I said. "I'm sure you both need rest. But call me if anything changes. I'll be here in a flash."

As I reached the door my dad called out, "You were going to say something, Rohan—just before the doctor walked in?"

"Oh yea," I said, turning back. "I wanted to ask if you remember that day we talked on the beach during our family vacation?"

"I most certainly do. I remember every word I said. Out of curiosity, do you remember what you promised me that day?"

I paused. And then it all came rushing back—the scent of the saltwater, the sky glowing in a thousand sunset hues. "I promised that I would pursue the things that brought me meaning and joy."

"Precisely," he said, with a kind grin.

"Dad, I have to confess—I forgot about that promise. That day. It got tucked away somewhere deep. But lately, I feel like I'm seeing signs again. I think I'm finding my way back. It's like the lens I use to see myself is shifting. And as it shifts, so does the path."

We both smiled.

"I love you both," I said, and stepped into the corridor.

***

The emergency ward had grown quieter, like life had taken a pause. The chaos—held at bay for a moment. These rare pockets of stillness give us a chance to breathe, to reflect, to prepare. We never know what's coming. But in these moments, we reconnect with peace—the kind that brings strength when we need it most.

So many lessons had been learned these past weeks, turning in my mind. Bringing their unique understanding: Peace is not happiness. Happiness is fleeting. Peace is the deeper truth. It transcends the daily rise and fall. It's not dependent on things going well—it's what comes when we align with our place in the cosmic journey and walk our true-life path...whatever that may mean to us, and us alone.

The double glass doors slid open, and the warm fresh air felt gentle and inviting. I decided to run home—I was dressed for it, after all.

A light rain began to fall from the pale grey sky.

As I crossed the parking lot, a man stepped out of his car and caught my eye. Tall and thin, with black framed glasses and a cigarette hanging from his lips. It was Dr. Chan. He closed his car door and walked toward the hospital, passing by me without the slightest hint of recognition. It felt strange seeing him.

Back in his office, I had felt so small—intimidated, desperate, dependent on his judgment. When I left, I'd been angry. But now? I felt no resentment. Maybe even understanding. He'd done what he thought was right. Maybe the medication would've worked. Maybe, had I been a different man, my decision to disregard his prescribed action, would have been a disaster. There was no way to know. All I knew was the path I had taken.

I smiled to myself. It sounded like something out of the Buddha's teachings. The middle way is the path of clarity. Of neutrality. Not indifference, but deeper understanding.

I realized I wasn't angry anymore because I was beginning to find that middle ground. I could see both sides. The middle path didn't mean silence or passivity—it meant wisdom in action. And I could finally understand: no one was ever going to save me. That was never their role. People can help. But this path? It's mine to walk.

I reached into my pocket and pulled out the card the taxi driver had given me: *No one saves us but ourselves. No one can and no one may. We ourselves must walk the path*—The Buddha.

I watched Dr. Chan disappear through the hospital doors. Then I turned and began to run—this time not too slow, and not too fast. Before I headed home, I had an important stop to make at the park.

The light rain felt liberating on my skin, and the dark clouds painted the afternoon sky, not fully telling whether a storm loomed or not. Either way it would be good.

I could feel a subtle presence. The shadow couldn't hide anymore—no longer looming out of sight…because I could see it now, right beside me.

About the Author

Sean Lewis is a storyteller drawn to the quiet places where the everyday meets the extraordinary. His fiction blends psychological depth, spiritual reflection, and a touch of magical realism—exploring how life's smallest moments often carry the greatest meaning.

After nearly three decades as a health and fitness coach, Sean turned his attention to writing, guided by the same belief he shared with his clients: transformation begins within. **The Journeyman: An Apprentice's Tale** is his debut novel, a deeply personal exploration of self-discovery, presence, and the paths we walk toward peace.

Sean lives in Canada, where he spends as much time as possible outdoors—often accompanied by his dog, Jaybe—finding inspiration in the magic hidden in plain sight.